MURDER
at the
ST. ALICE

FSC
www.fsc.org

MIX
Paper from
responsible sources
FSC® C016245

ENVIRONMENTAL BENEFITS STATEMENT

Coteau Books saved the following resources by
printing the pages of this book on chlorine free paper
made with 100% post-consumer waste.

TREES	WATER	ENERGY	SOLID WASTE	GREENHOUSE GASES
8	650	3	28	3,530
FULLY GROWN	GALLONS	MILLION BTUs	POUNDS	POUNDS

Environmental impact estimates were made using the Environmental Paper Network
Paper Calculator 4.0. For more information visit www.papercalculator.org.

MURDER

at the

ST. ALICE

BECKY CITRA

COTEAU BOOKS

Edited by Kathy Stinson
Designed by Tania Craan
Photographs courtesy Agassiz-Harrison Historical Society
Printed and bound in Canada

Library and Archives Canada Cataloguing in Publication

Citra, Becky, author
    Murder at the St. Alice / Becky Citra.
Issued in print and electronic formats.
ISBN 978-1-55050-962-5 (softcover).--ISBN 978-1-55050-963-2 (PDF).--
ISBN 978-1-55050-964-9 (HTML).--ISBN 978-1-55050-965-6 (Kindle)
I. Title.
PS8555.I87M87 2018   jC813'.54   C2018-902748-7
                                               C2018-902749-5

Library of Congress Control Number: 2017962855

COTEAU
BOOKS

2517 Victoria Avenue
Regina, Saskatchewan
Canada S4P 0T2
www.coteaubooks.com

Available in Canada from:
Publishers Group Canada
2440 Viking Way
Richmond, British Columbia
Canada V6V 1N2

10 9 8 7 6 5 4 3 2 1

Coteau Books gratefully acknowledges the financial support of its publishing program by: the Saskatchewan Arts Board, The Canada Council for the Arts, the Government of Saskatchewan through Creative Saskatchewan, the City of Regina. We further acknowledge the [financial] support of the Government of Canada. Nous reconnaissons l'appui [financier] du gouvernement du Canada.

For Bev

THE ST. ALICE HOTEL

1908

Chapter One

"I don't usually hire girls without experience," said Mrs. Bannerman on my first day at the St. Alice Hotel.

She eyed me across the table in the small stuffy housekeeper's room at the end of the hallway behind the kitchen and dining room. She wore a black dress, closed tightly at the neck with a cameo.

My sad lonely reference lay in the middle of the table – a badly spelled letter from our neighbour in Victoria, Mrs. Stokes, saying that I had minded her five children for over a year (two sets of twins and a colicky baby, all under the age of six.) She said I was a *respectable girl* and that she would *miss me sorely.*

Mrs. Bannerman stared at the letter and sniffed. My heart sank. Was she going to send me back on the next train?

She had another piece of paper in front of her, my carefully written application. She glanced down at it.

"You were born in Toronto, Charlotte, and moved to Victoria six years ago?"

"Yes, Ma'am."

"You're fifteen years old?"

"Almost sixteen."

"Your parents are deceased and you live with a Miss Virginia Lane?"

"Yes, Ma'am. My Great Aunt Ginny."

"And you got as far as grade nine with your schooling?"

"I'm going back. As soon as I save enough money."

Mrs. Bannerman studied me.

"I usually go to Victoria and Vancouver to interview my staff. But things have happened very quickly. One of the girls had to leave unexpectedly."

She'd been sacked, I guessed. What had she done? Splattered gravy on one of those fusty old gentlemen I had spotted in the parlour on my way in? Tipped over a coffee pot on the ladies' playing cards?

"Very well," said Mrs. Bannerman. "I'm hiring you as a waitress in our dining room but you will be expected to perform other duties as well."

"Thank you!"

"If you have any problems, come directly to me, not the hotel manager. Mr. Brown doesn't have time to deal with domestic matters. You'll be sharing a room with Lizzie. She's been waitressing here for a year. I've instructed her to teach you the routine."

Mrs. Bannerman stood up and handed me a stack of folded clothes. I was surprised how short she was, just past my shoulder. "Your uniforms. One for the daytime and one for the dinner hour. I expect your cuffs and collars to be cleaned and starched every night." She placed a book on top of the stack. The title on the brown cover said *The Up-To-Date Waitress*. "You will find this a great source of information and inspiration."

"Yes, Ma'am."

"You can start tomorrow morning. I've told the cook Mrs. Wiggs to expect you at six-thirty sharp. The staff eat in the staff dining room at six."

"Yes, Ma'am."

"Lizzie is waiting for you in the kitchen. She'll take you up to your room. I noticed you came in the front door. Staff use the back entrance to the hotel and the back staircase at all times. The front door is for guests unless you are serving refreshments on the verandah. The annex behind the hotel, where the young men live, is strictly out of bounds."

Mrs. Bannerman fixed me with cool grey eyes. "I want to make it absolutely clear that there is to be no fraternizing with the guests."

She sat down again and ruffled through a stack of papers. Without looking up, she said, "You're dismissed."

I shifted the uniforms and book to one arm and picked up my small suitcase. I almost danced out the door. The advertisement in the *British Colonist* described the hotel as a jewel in the wilderness, nestled on the shores of beautiful Harrison Lake, surrounded by majestic mountains. It screamed *adventure!*

I set down my suitcase so I could shut the door. "You'll have to do something about your hair," said Mrs. Bannerman.

Lizzie took me up the back stairs to our room. It was small with a slanted ceiling, two iron beds, two dressers and a washstand with a jug.

I put my suitcase on the floor.

"My bed's the one by the window," said Lizzie. She was tall and freckly with shiny brown hair. "I have to go straight back to the kitchen and there's so much to talk about. Are you awfully tired?"

"Yes. And grubby."

"Well, one thing the St. Alice has is plenty of hot water. They pump it from the hot springs. You can have all the baths you want. There's a bathroom at the end of the hall. And I do love your hair!"

My thick red hair had fallen loose and frizzed in the misty air. "It's a disaster," I said cheerfully.

"I'll be back as soon as I can," said Lizzie.

I stripped out of my brown travelling suit, right down to my undergarments. I opened my suitcase and took out a photograph of my parents in a slim gold frame. I set it on the dresser beside my bed. A warm bath? Heaven.

⁓

I sank up to my chin, washing away the dust and grime. I tried to sort out my impressions of my journey. I had never been away from Victoria before. Early that morning, I had crossed the strait from Vancouver Island, in the steamship *The Queen of Victoria*, and then I rode on the train up the valley. An omnibus with the words "Harrison Hot Springs" in green letters on the front met me at the CPR station in the tiny town of Agassiz.

I had always wanted to ride in a motorized vehicle!

Three hotel guests, a gentleman and two ladies with magnificent feathered hats, sat at the back. I perched on the edge of my seat behind the driver in a spiffy blue uniform who introduced himself as Frank. We bumped over the six miles of rough wagon road between towering dark trees and scattered farms.

I gasped at my first glimpse of the huge lake, slate grey under the cloudy skies, and the three-storey green-and-white building with the sweeping verandahs that was the St. Alice Hotel. Frank laughed. "It's only the end of April," he said. "Wait 'til you see this place in the summer!"

I splashed water on my face and scrubbed my cheeks. I thought of all the questions I was dying to ask Lizzie.

⁓

When Lizzie got back, I was lying on my bed reading *The Up-To-Date Waitress*. I read bits out loud while she changed into her nightdress.

"A waitress needs to be quick and light of foot; thus youth and a trim fig-ure, not too large, are the first requisites in one who wishes to make a success of the calling."

Lizzie snorted.

"Her first duty in regard to everything she touches is to 'keep it straight'. What on earth does that mean?"

"The forks and knives. Line them up properly. There's all kinds of rules about setting the tables." Lizzie picked up the frame on my dresser. "Are these your parents?"

"Yes."

"They look so kind."

I already felt like I could confide in Lizzie. "They died when I was ten. Their carriage was hit by a runaway horse on Yonge Street in Toronto."

"How awful. I don't have a photograph of my family. There's lots of us. I have three sisters and four brothers. We live in Chilliwack."

Lizzie climbed into bed. "I was going to write about you coming but I'd rather talk. Victoria. That's such a long way. I've never been but I want to."

"Do you write every day?" I said.

"Yes. I'm going to be an author."

"I'm going to be a pharmacist."

We smiled at each other. I knew we were going to be great friends.

Chapter Two

Lizzie said she heard me say, "Tines turned upward," in the middle of the night.

While we were dressing, I asked her to test me on my new-found knowledge but she just laughed.

I had stayed up half the night studying *The Up-To-Date Waitress*. The hotel had electricity (it came from a steam plant near the Bath House, Lizzie explained) but no one had bothered about the maids' rooms and I had read by spluttering candlelight.

My head was crowded with tips. *At the point of the knife, set a tumbler of water...at the point of the fork, set a small plate of butter...plates, knives, forks and spoons are set half an inch from the edge of the table.*

Or was it an inch?

"Let me straighten your cap," said Lizzie. "You've pinned it on crooked."

"It's my hair," I moaned. "It's too springy."

Puzzling forks and annoying hair. My stomach was a tangled knot.

I took a shuddery breath and smoothed down my apron.

"Print dress and plain apron for the morning and lunch. Black dress and fancy apron for dinner," I said. *"On all occasions she is to be neatly dressed and manicured, calm and unruffled."*

Lizzie threw her pillow at me.

⌒⌒

Lizzie and I went down to the kitchen together. An enormous woman, wrapped in acres of white apron, was lifting a pan of golden biscuits out of the oven of a huge black range. Kind blue eyes beamed at me from a face glowing red from the heat. "I'm Mrs. Wiggs."

"I'm Charlotte."

"Well, we can certainly use some more help around here. Can't we, girls?"

Four girls stopped what they were doing and stared at me. Mrs. Wiggs introduced them.

"This is Ina and Flora. They're sisters."

Two skinny girls, who I guessed to be about eight and twelve, gawked at me.

"They come from a big family in Agassiz. They're our scullery maids but they do a little bit of everything in a pinch," said Mrs. Wiggs. "Don't you, dears?"

Ina and Flora bobbed their heads.

"This is Annie, our other waitress. She just comes for the day. She lives on a farm on the Agassiz road."

Annie was chubby with blond hair. She smiled and I smiled back.

"Glenys, our kitchen maid."

Glenys was slicing a large loaf of brown bread on a big wooden table in the middle of the kitchen. She had big hands like a man and patches of dreadful acne on her cheeks. She must have hated it because underneath she was quite pretty. She gave me a long cool look and then went back to her slicing. Lizzie rolled her eyes.

"Have you had your breakfast, Charlotte?" said Mrs. Wiggs.

"Yes, thank you."

Lizzie and I had sipped mugs of tea and ploughed through bowls of oatmeal at the long table in the staff dining room, in the company of a few sleepy-eyed maids and two boys in working clothes who smelled of horse.

Mrs. Wiggs clapped her hands. "Everyone back to work. We've got hungry guests coming in an hour and the food won't cook itself. Ina and Flora, you get onto those pots and mind you scrub them out properly. Glenys, it's time to get the sausages on. Annie and Lizzie, you show Charlotte how to lay a proper table. And Charlotte?"

"Yes, Mrs. Wiggs."

"Ask Lizzie to give you a lesson with your cap."

∾

Annie and Lizzie decided that I would start with three tables.

"We'll give you Mr. Paisley," said Lizzie. "He always sits at that little corner table by the window. He's ninety-one and he lives at the hotel. He has his own private nurse. I swear you'll fall madly in love with him. We all have."

"Who else would be good?" said Annie.

"Some of the regulars. They're the guests who come every year and stay for weeks and weeks, Char. They come to take the waters from the hot springs."

"The widows, then," said Annie. "They don't mind if you get their orders mixed up. They like this table right in the middle of things."

"And the Howards," finished Lizzie. "Americans from San Francisco. They're loads of fun and easy to wait on."

I pulled my eyes away from the wide windows that looked out on the lake and mountains. I gazed around the room with its glittering chandeliers, sea of tables covered in dazzling white cloths and huge sideboards gleaming with silver and rows of sparkling glasses. I imagined it full of guests. My nerves came flying back.

We set out knives, forks and spoons, snowy white napkins, little plates with perfect balls of chilled butter, pots of jam, jugs of cream and glass bowls of cut sugar. I abandoned *The Up-To-Date Waitress* and just followed what Lizzie and Annie did.

Each time I went back through the swinging doors, the amount of food kept growing – platters of bacon, sausages and ham that were popped into the warming cupboard, eggs sizzling in huge black frying pans, a pot of Cream of Wheat burbling at the back of the range, glass bowls of pale green melons, trays of cheese scones and muffins bursting with currants.

We put the finishing touches on the tables.

"A water jug for the Howards," said Annie.

"Don't forget Mr. Paisley likes blackberry jam," said Lizzie.

"Here they come," said Annie.

"Ready?" said Lizzie.

∼∾c

A cheery-faced woman in a nurse's uniform brought Mr. Paisley to his table. He was folded over and as frail as a sparrow with tufts of white down on his pale freckled head. She settled him on a pillow while I hovered beside them, afraid that he might topple off.

"I'll be back for you in an hour," she said. "And look, you've got a pretty new waitress to look after you today."

Mr. Paisley reached out a thin hand, dotted with brown spots, and patted her on her bottom as she left. He leered at me. "Where have you been all my life, gorgeous?"

He dithered between boiled eggs and bacon or fried potatoes and sausages and finally settled on toast and tea, which I suspected was what he had every morning.

∼∾c

Two of the widows were thin like twigs. Two were stout with amazing bosoms. Their dresses were beautiful – turquoise, lavender, bottle green and copper – decorated with tucks, lace and embroidery. Their names were Mrs. Clegg, Mrs. Hawthorne, Mrs. Bice and Mrs. Webster. I gave Mrs. Bice the sausages and cheese scones and Mrs. Webster the bacon and currant muffins.

Mrs. Bice gaped at her sausages. "Oh, my dear..."

"It's backwards, isn't it?" My face blazed. "I'm so sorry."

As I switched the plates, Mrs. Webster winked at me. "No harm done. Tell me, Charlotte, I hope you're not homesick."

"At the St. Alice?" interrupted Mrs. Clegg. "Of course she's not. Now Charlotte, you try and guess how many years the four of us have been coming here."

"Four?" I worried that they would keep me at their table chatting and I wouldn't get everything done.

"Eight!" said Mrs. Webster triumphantly.

"That's amazing!" Mumbling something about cream and sugar, I made my escape.

The dining room was filling up with guests. How did Lizzie and Annie do it? *Calm and unruffled, calm and unruffled,* I whispered. Lizzie passed me carrying a tray loaded sky-high with plates and I remembered how *The Up-To-Date Waitress* sternly advised no more than five plates at a time.

"It saves another trip to the kitchen," Lizzie said, as she pushed against the swinging door with her shoulder. "I'm the Queen of Shortcuts. Mrs. Bannerman is suspicious but she's never caught me yet."

⁓⁘

Mr. and Mrs. Howard had the full breakfast. They chatted enthusiastically about their plans for the day. It came down to fishing or the steamboat excursion up the lake. The steamboat won and they asked me to order a picnic lunch from the kitchen.

I sped between my tables. Fresh tea for the widows. Another rack of toast for the Howards. Rearrange Mr. Paisley's pillow. Fill the water jugs. Fetch some more butter from the kitchen.

Mr. Paisley was the last of my guests to leave. By the end of his meal, he had scattered crusts of toast and blobs of blackberry jam everywhere. He slurped down the dregs of his tea, glanced at the dining room door and said, "Here comes my warden."

He gave me a jammy smile. "You doing anything after work?"

～✹C

The room service trays were next. They were lined up in a row, each covered with a white linen cloth. Six trays were for guests in the hotel and a seventh tray for someone called Mr. Pincer who lived in a cottage on the hotel grounds.

"He likes his eggs runny," said sour-faced Glenys.

"Firm," said Mrs. Wiggs.

"Crisp bacon," said Glenys.

Mrs. Wiggs frowned. "Not too crisp."

Lizzie finally headed out with his breakfast through the back door of the kitchen.

A maid appeared at the other door with a message for Mrs. Wiggs. "Mrs. Bannerman wants to see you right away, Mrs. Wiggs. Something about changing the soup for lunch."

"She should try running a kitchen at the busiest time of the day" muttered Mrs. Wiggs. "Mr. Wiggs says he doesn't know why I put up with it."

Ina and Flora were busy washing stacks of dishes in the scullery and Annie was still in the dining room, finishing up with a few guests. I was alone in the kitchen with Glenys, who was rolling out pastry on a wooden board. "Can I do anything to help?"

Glenys's hands went still. "You could do the tea for the trays. The tea's in that black canister with the gold label on it, and the kettles have just boiled."

Aunt Ginny had taught me how to make a good pot of tea. I poured hot water into the six pots to warm them and then poured it out again. I scooped the dark loose tea from the canister into the tea balls, put one in each pot and filled it to the top with boiling water and put on the lid. I had just finished the last pot when Mrs. Wiggs appeared.

"If you ask me, you can't go wrong with a bowl of plain tomato soup. Who does she – What on earth are you doing, Charlotte?"

"The tea for the trays," I stammered.

"The trays don't go up for another twenty minutes! The tea can't sit that long. It'll be stew!" Her eyes rested on the black canister which was still open. "Heaven help us! You've used the special afternoon tea. We never use that for breakfast and now it's all going to be wasted. What were you thinking?"

Glenys kept her eyes down and crimped the edge of a pie.

Chapter Three

Lizzie, Annie and I had polished mounds of silver and were in the staff dining room having tea before the lunch time rush. At the end of the table, Frank from the omnibus was deep in conversation with a grey-haired man in faded overalls. Lizzie had told me he was Mr. Bains, the gardener.

"I'd put my Maisie up against your new-fangled contraption any day of the week," said Mr. Bains.

Frank snorted. "Got to move with the times, Albert. Now you listen to me..."

"Glenys hates me," I said.

"It's not you," said Lizzie. "It's because of Fleur. Glenys'd hate anyone who took Fleur's place."

"Who's Fleur?"

Annie leaned closer. "The last waitress. Mrs. Bannerman sacked her for..." She glanced down the table at Frank and Mr. Bains. "For being in the family way."

"Pregnant," said Lizzie.

"You should have heard Mrs. Bannerman telling her off," said Annie. "You could hear her clear down to the kitchen. *Have you no shame?*"

"Fleur was Glenys's best friend," said Lizzie. "They did everything together."

"Her only friend," added Annie. "We all madly tried to guess who the father was. The bellboys even laid bets."

"Poor Fleur," I said. "Did you ever find out who it was?"

Lizzie shook her head. "She was always going back and forth to Vancouver. She must have met someone there."

"I wish I could have seen Mrs. Wiggs' face," said Annie. "She hoards that tea like it's gold."

"Do you think Mrs. Bannerman will take it out of my wages?"

"Mrs. Wiggs won't tell," said Lizzie.

"What should I do about Glenys?"

"Stay out of her way," said Annie.

"Right," said Lizzie. "The last thing you need is Glenys for an enemy."

∾

I muddled through lunch and afternoon tea without making any really awful mistakes. As I handed out plates of shrimp sandwiches cut into tiny triangles and dainty iced cakes, Mrs. Bannerman's eagle eye followed me around the room.

"I think I can manage another table or two at dinner," I told Lizzie.

"Maybe. But first you have to meet Mr. Pincer, the dinner cook."

I remembered the fuss over his breakfast. "How bad can he be?"

"Horrible," said Annie. "And you're supposed to call him a *chef.* He used to cook in a fancy restaurant in New York."

"He's not going to order *me* around," I said.

"Just wait," said Annie.

∾

On my break, I set out for the village, which was just a scattering of cottages. There were two or three larger houses, one with a garden of bright tulips and a sign on a post that said "Dr. Herman", a little white church and a store called *Inkman's.* I admired the Indian baskets in the window and then went inside to buy some washing powder for my cuffs and collars and a packet of needles and thread.

Tools, coils of rope, axes and lanterns hung from the low ceiling. Behind a long wooden counter, shelves were crowded with an assortment of tins and boxes. At one end a girl stood, a pencil in her hand, studying a paper covered with rows of numbers. She had black hair and tan skin and she wore a beautiful beaded necklace.

"Are you new here?" she said.

"My first day. Can you tell?"

"The girls don't wear their caps when they come to the village."

"Good advice. But if I take it off, I'll never get it back on straight."

She smiled. She was quick to find my purchases and wrap them in brown paper.

On my way out, I spotted a rack of postcards tucked into a corner. The cards made me think about Aunt Ginny and how I must write to her.

I was flipping through the cards for one of the St. Alice when the bell tinkled. I peeked around the rack and saw Colonel Mitterand, a guest from the hotel. He was a short heavy man wearing an old-fashioned tweed suit. His black hair shone with oil and he had the biggest pair of mutton chop sideburns I'd ever seen.

Lizzie had pointed him out to me at breakfast. "No one wants to wait on him," she'd said. "He complains about everything."

Colonel Mitterand gazed around the store.

"Can I help you?" said the girl.

"Missy have ink?" he said.

He slowly spelled it out. "I.N.K. You understand? Ink?"

Did he think she didn't understand English? I abandoned the postcards and slipped out the door.

A wagon rumbled past with Mrs. Wiggs sitting in the front beside a man wearing suspenders and a brown hat. Mr. Wiggs, I guessed. The scullery maids Flora and little Ina were in the back. They waved wildly. "Charlotte!" they shouted.

Two loggers with trousers cut off below their knees and high-topped boots were loading supplies onto a boat at the end of the long dock. A canoe glided by with an Indian in the back surrounded by bundles, and farther out a white sailboat scudded across the water.

Time to face Mr. Pincer.

~oc

Mr. Pincer wore a tall white chef's hat and a white jacket with two rows of buttons. He had tiny teeth and black eyes like marbles.

He flew around the kitchen, peering into pots.

"Salt in the water before you put in the potatoes," he said to Glenys. "We've gone over that enough times. And I want the asparagus served cold with the trout...Girl! Why are you taking out the grapefruit now?"

Lizzie jumped.

"Grapefruit clears the palate *after* the entrée."

Mr. Pincer stared at me. "Have I seen you before? You've got to move faster. The guests expect their butter *with* their dinner rolls."

Annie passed me in the swinging doorway. "We warned you."

I set an empty tray on the kitchen table. My feet ached.

Mr. Pincer loomed over Glenys. "Why are you heating the cucumber soup? It's a *chilled* soup!"

Glenys's cheeks flamed. Mr. Pincer tipped the pot over the sink and poured it out.

"Ruined!"

~oc

While we were getting ready for bed, Lizzie pranced around our room. "That's cayenne pepper, not black pepper! French onion soup is served in *heated* bowls!"

"Don't make me laugh. I'm too tired." I hung up my uniform and dropped into bed.

"But you survived. You did really well. I dropped a whole tray of omelettes my first day."

"Mmm." My eyes shut.

From a million miles away, I heard Lizzie say, "I'll rinse out your cuffs and collar."

Chapter Four

A few days later, Mr. Doyle was due to arrive.

Mr. Bains spent the morning trimming the shrubs under the front windows. Mrs. Wiggs rushed around the kitchen making Mr. Doyle's favourite raspberry trifle and lemon tarts.

"He's a real gentleman," she said. "Right as rain, he's here every year on the first of May."

"And a great tipper," added the bellboy Clarence.

It was a cool afternoon but sunny, and many of the guests were having their tea at the small round tables on the verandah. I was busy handing out tartan blankets to the widows playing bridge. Frank pulled the omnibus up to the front of the hotel.

Mike, the boy who helped Frank with the omnibus, scrambled on top where the suitcases were strapped and started undoing buckles.

At the widows' table Mrs. Clegg said, "At last! Jacob Doyle! Now we'll have some fun."

Mr. Brown stood at the bottom of the stairs, waiting to greet the guests. A grey haired man helped a sweet looking old lady off the omnibus. They were followed by two young couples carrying tennis rackets in their cases.

Next, an elegant lady in a fitted green suit and a bowler hat with bronze pheasant feathers stepped down, accompanied by a girl with a rabbity face and eyes that darted about.

"Good Lord," said Mrs. Hawthorne. "That's Miranda Chisholm. I didn't read anything on the society page about her coming here."

"I've never seen her at the St. Alice before," said Mrs. Bice.

Mr. Brown strode forward. "Mrs. Chisholm, welcome to the St. Alice! Clarence, escort Mrs. Chisholm to the lobby."

The last guest off was a stout man with a reddish face, ginger hair combed straight back from his forehead and a magnificent sweeping moustache.

"Mr. Doyle!" said Fred.

Mr. Doyle clapped Fred on the shoulder. He shook Mr. Brown's hand and started up the stairs. Colonel Mitterand, at a table at the far end of the verandah, lurched to his feet. "Doyle!" he shouted.

Mr. Doyle stopped.

A hush fell over the verandah.

"We've been waiting for you," said Colonel Mitterand.

Mr. Doyle nodded. "Mitterand."

Colonel Mitterand looked around. "We were great pals in the Boer War, your Mr. Doyle and I. In the same regiment. But we don't talk about those days, do we Jacob?"

A muscle twitched in Mr. Doyle's cheek. "Damn you," he said under his breath.

Then Mrs. Webster said in a loud clear voice, "Mr. Doyle, can we count on you to join us for dinner?"

"Perhaps tomorrow," said Mr. Doyle.

Colonel Mitterand slumped back into his chair. "The great Jacob Doyle," he said, attacking his scone with gusto.

I wasn't expecting to see a narrow cot taking up one corner of our room and the girl from the omnibus perched on the edge of it.

"This is Beatrice," said Lizzie, in her usual spot by the window, writing. "She's Mrs. Chadworth's maid."

"Not Mrs. Chadworth," said Beatrice. "Mrs. *Chisholm.* I told you twice already."

I treasured sharing a room with Lizzie. "How long are you staying?"

"Dunno." Beatrice chewed on a fingernail.

I unbuttoned my shoes and flopped on my bed. We had a short break before the dinner rush and I wasn't going to waste one second of it.

"You must have heard of Mrs. Chisholm," said Beatrice. "You know? High society in Victoria? She has that huge mansion with the turrets on top in Rockland."

"Never been to Victoria," said Lizzie.

"Oh," said Beatrice.

I closed my eyes.

"That's interesting, though," added Lizzie.

"She was married to a judge," said Beatrice. "He died four years ago."

"That's sad," said Lizzie.

"It's terrible. Mrs. Chisholm misses him awfully. But she's still the president of the Victoria Chamber Music Society. And last week she had a fancy dinner party and the Lieutenant Governor and his wife came."

"Shouldn't you be helping her?" said Lizzie. "Unpacking her suitcases or something?"

"She's resting. She doesn't want to be disturbed. She might be getting a migraine."

"Take her some ice wrapped in a cloth," I said.

"I said she *might* be getting a migraine."

"Gotta go." Lizzie snapped her book shut. "I need to run up to *Inkman's* before dinner. See you, Char."

Five minutes of peace. That's all I wanted.

"You wouldn't believe Mrs. Chisholm's dining room," said Beatrice. "She has enough silver settings for twenty guests."

I lay perfectly still.

I heard Beatrice breathing, the cot squeak, a huge sigh and then the door shut.

～

That night, the guests took ages over their coffees and liqueurs.

Annie and Lizzie were already in the kitchen, having a quick cup of tea before the final clean up. I had two tables left. One was a party of six with Colonel Mitterand droning on about the Boer War. Mrs. Chisholm sat alone at a table in the corner, looking exhausted with her coffee untouched.

I offered her a cup from a fresh pot. Up close, she was lovely, with creamy skin and fine lines around her hazel eyes. She wore a silk evening gown the colour of milky tea.

"I'm going up in a few minutes," she said.

I drifted over to the Colonel's table with my empty tray.

"It's not right," said a man called Mr. Timmins. He had a pale face with strands of black hair combed over his bald spot. I'd seen him limping in the garden. A riding accident, Lizzie had said.

His face flushed. "We don't understand the insane. We punish them instead of trying to help them. It's criminal."

"My good man," declared Colonel Mitterand. The glass of dark red port in his hand swayed. "Mary Ann Ansell murdered her *own sister!* What can be more heinous than that?"

"She was not of right mind," insisted Mr. Timmins.

"A sorry excuse."

"The details," cried Mrs. Howard, who was seated next to Mr. Timmins. "Give us the details and we shall be the judge."

"A colleague of mine defended her at the trial in London," said Mr. Timmins.

I gave up pretending to clear the table.

"Mary Ann was twenty years old. She was a maid in London in a townhouse on Sloane Square near Buckingham Palace. Her sister was a mental patient at Leavesden Asylum. Mary Ann sent her a cake – "

"Laced with rat poison." Colonel Mitterand pounded the table. "Cyanide!"

"Good God," said Mr. Howard.

"It was in all the papers," said Colonel Mitterand. "She bought the cake at a local shop and injected it with the poison."

"How dreadful," said a stout woman called Mrs. Peel.

"In the middle of the trial she broke while on the stand and confessed," said Colonel Mitterand.

"It wasn't her fault," protested Mr. Timmins. "She heard voices."

"What happened to her?" said Mrs. Peel.

"Hanged." Colonel Mitterand picked up a breadstick and snapped it in two. "Like that."

At her table in the corner, Mrs. Chisholm rose to her feet. Before my astonished eyes, she crumpled to the floor in a dead faint.

Chapter Five

I ran to get Mrs. Bannerman.

When we got back, Mrs. Chisholm had revived and was sitting on a chair, her head down. The guests were milling around her.

"She needs air," said Mr. Timmins, his hand resting on her shoulder. "I must insist you all move back and give the lady some room."

"Smelling salts." Mrs. Peel waved a small brown bottle. "I never travel without them."

"Thank you, Mrs. Peel," said Mr. Timmins firmly, "but that's not necessary."

"Damn bad show," said Colonel Mitterand.

Mrs. Chisholm whispered in Mr. Timmins's ear. He nodded and turned to the guests. "Mrs. Chisholm asks everyone to return to their dinners. She apologizes for this interruption."

"I'll take Mrs. Chisholm to her room," said Mrs. Bannerman. "Charlotte, make a pot of hot tea and bring it up."

The rooms in the hotel were named after great cities and Mrs. Chisholm was in *Venice* on the second floor.

Beatrice, her cheeks pink, was waiting in the hall. "Now look what's happened! Why Mrs. Chisholm ever got it in her head to come to a hotel in the middle of nowhere, I just don't know. I said we should go on a cruise to San Francisco. You meet the poshest people on a cruise. But no, her mind was set on coming here."

"The tea's getting cold," I said.

Beatrice grabbed the tray. "I'm going to be up all night."

I hurried back to our room. Lizzie had unpinned her long brown hair and was sitting on the edge of her bed, brushing it.

"You'll never guess what happened at dinner!" I said.

∼∾∁

In the morning, Mr. Doyle asked for a breakfast tray. He hadn't come down to dinner the night before either.

"He always eats breakfast in his room," said Mrs. Wiggs. "He wants tea and toast and two boiled eggs. You fix up his tray, Charlotte. Don't worry about jam. He brings his own special marmalade and keeps it in his room. He has a few persnickety habits and that's one of them."

Mr. Doyle was in *Paris*, at the end of the hallway on the same floor as Mrs. Chisholm and the Howards. I set the tray on the floor in front of his door and knocked.

"Come in," he called.

He was dressed and seated by the open window. A fresh breeze blew the curtain back.

"Thank you, my dear," he said, as I set the tray in front of him. "You're new here, aren't you? What is your name?"

"Charlotte."

He stared harder at me.

"Is something wrong? Is my cap on crooked?"

He threw back his head and roared with laughter, which made me laugh too. "Not at all. Your cap is charming. You remind me of my sister when she was young. You look just like her. It's uncanny."

He picked up his knife. "You're going to find me an awful nuisance asking for a breakfast tray every morning."

"Oh no, sir. Lots of the guests have trays in their rooms. I've got to go back and get Mrs. Chisholm's breakfast next."

"Ah, Miranda Chisholm. She's a lovely lady. I knew Judge Chisholm well. We were both members of the Union Club in Victoria and we often had lunch together."

"She fainted in the dining room last night."

"How distressing."

"Some of the guests were talking about a murder and she just fainted."

"I expect she was tired from her long journey."

I left Mr. Doyle slathering marmalade from a big round jar on a piece of toast.

～～

"Mr. Wiggs says the weather's changing tomorrow," said Mrs. Wiggs. "You girls should leave the silver for now and get outside and enjoy the sunshine for half an hour."

Mrs. Bannerman caught me as I was flying out the back door. "Take this to the Bath House." She handed me a stiff cardboard folder with the words *St. Alice Hotel* in gold letters on the front. "It's confidential so don't give it to one of those scatterbrained boys. It's to go straight to George."

I peeked as soon as I was outside. It was very dull, just a list of the guests who had come to the hotel for the healing waters. I spotted Mr. Doyle's name at the bottom, with *arthritis in knees* penciled beside it.

The Bath House was a ten minute walk along a path that followed the lake shore, winding between lush ferns and towering cedar trees. Guests in white bathrobes strolled past me in the sunshine. Mr. Paisley inched his way along the path, clutching his nurse.

As I got closer, I saw steam rising from the roof of the Bath House. It was a two-storey wooden structure built on piles, with a plunge pool and lots of vapour baths and ordinary baths with exotic names like *Hades* and *Purgatory* and *Vesuvius*.

George, a man from Ethiopia, stood by the door, smoking a cigarette. He was one of the tallest men I'd ever seen. I had already been to the Bath House a few times and had gotten used to his black skin. He had a flashing white smile and huge muscles on his arms. Lizzie and I guessed it was from pumping lake water to fill the big barrels used to cool the water from the hot spring.

"Hello there, Charlotte," he called.

"Hello, George." I delivered the folder and we chatted for a few minutes, while George insisted I drink a glass of the mineral water.

On the way back, I stopped to watch a tennis match on the lawn beside the hotel. The two young couples who had arrived yesterday were playing and hurling insults at each other. I would have loved to try my hand at the game but *The Up-To-Date Waitress* would never approve.

I pulled myself away from the tennis and ran inside to the kitchen. Mr. Bains, the gardener, wearing overalls and black rubber boots, was holding a wicker basket full of small round white objects that looked like dirty golf balls.

"Mushrooms," he grunted. "Puffballs." He dumped out the basket in the middle of the long work table.

"For lands' sake, you could have at least put some newspapers down," grumbled Mrs. Wiggs. "You're getting dirt everywhere."

We all stared at the mushrooms.

"Puffballs," Mr. Bains pronounced again.

Mrs. Wiggs poked one. "Mr. Wiggs is fond of mushroom soup."

"Found them behind the greenhouse."

"Death angels, most likely," said Glenys. "My granny thought she was eating puffballs. Turned out to be death angels. They gave her seizures." A hint of a smile slid across her spotty face. "A week later she dropped dead."

Mr. Bains stuck out his chin. "I know my mushrooms. Puffballs."

"I ain't eating them," said Flora. She and Ina had crept out of the scullery to see.

"Take them back outside and get rid of them, Mr. Bains," said Mrs. Wiggs. "I'll take no chances of a guest being poisoned. Not at the St. Alice."

Chapter Six

On the weekend, a real live suffragette came to the St. Alice.

Gertie met her first. I didn't know what a suffragette was until Gertie told us during our morning break.

"It's someone who fights for women to have the vote," she said.

I'd never thought about women voting before.

"Her name is Abigail Pomphrey-Jones."

"Posh," said Rachel.

"She doesn't act posh," said Gertie. "When I went in to clean her room she was in her pajamas and drinking coffee in bed! She's come all the way from London to stay with her sister Sarah in Vancouver. Sarah's here too."

"Are there lots of suffragettes in London?" asked Annie.

"Hundreds. Abigail belongs to a group called The Women's Freedom League. She showed me her card. She goes to meetings and marches and everything. Her father sent her to Canada to get her away from the bad influence of other suffragettes. But Abigail says it's no use. Her mind is made up to be a suffragette and that's that."

"I can't wait to see her!" I said.

"She wears trousers!" added Gertie. "I saw them hanging over the back of her chair."

To my great disappointment, Abigail wasn't wearing her trousers when she and her sister came to lunch but instead a plain navy skirt and white blouse. She barely looked any older than me but she led a much more adventurous life.

Lucky Lizzie waited on their table, while I sorted out the widows' orders. Abigail glanced my way and caught me staring. She gave me a great wink.

I was so busy daydreaming about becoming a suffragette that I completely mixed up Mr. Paisley's lamb chops and Mr. Timmins's plaice (they were very nice about it), and I forgot all about Colonel Mitterand's second helping of trifle (*he* was not nice at all).

~∾c

I didn't actually speak to Abigail until the next day. I was walking back to the hotel from fetching some tooth powder at *Inkman's*, thinking that I would stop at my favourite bench and watch the comings and goings on the dock. Abigail was there ahead of me, poring over a newspaper. She was, at last, wearing trousers, a man's motor coat and no hat, her hair twisted into a long braid.

I prayed that Mrs. Bannerman wasn't looking out an upstairs window, and plunked down beside her. "Hello." I smiled. " I'm Charlotte."

She closed her newspaper and stuck out her hand. "Abigail."

I glanced at the bold title on her newspaper: *The Vote*.

"I didn't mean to interrupt you."

"You're not. I'm just trying to keep up-to-date on what's happening while I'm gone."

I grinned.

"Did I say something funny?"

"It's just the words *up-to-date*. I've got this book called *The Up-To-Date Waitress*. It's full of rules and I'm supposed to remember them all."

"Is it dreadful?"

"Horrible."

I described a few passages. She laughed, then frowned. "It only goes to show what's wrong with this world. We're treated as if we have no brains at all. Oh you poor thing, I can't imagine being a waitress." She grabbed my arm. "How tactless of me. I don't know when to shut up."

"Don't worry. I won't be a waitress forever. I'm saving my money to go back to school and become a pharmacist."

"Bravo! Will you keep working if you get married?"

"I'll decide then."

"Terrific! I'll always work. I'm going to be a journalist. Right now, I'm figuring out how to get back to London by June. There's going to be a huge march in the streets. There'll be thousands of us demanding our rights. The Women's Freedom League are going and the WSPU. That's the Women's Social and Political Union."

She pulled a crumpled paper from the pocket of her coat and smoothed it out. It was a poster of a woman striding along a street, blowing a bugle, with a long sword strapped to her side. At the top it said WOMEN'S SUFFRAGE MARCH AND MASS MEETING SATURDAY JUNE 13.

"I've got to be there," said Abigail. "To hell with Papa and his antiquated ideas."

"It sounds thrilling!"

"I'm not going to let my family stop me. My sister Sarah is as ignorant as Papa. But I think she's starting to listen to me. And I'll make the best of things while I'm here. Try to educate Canadian women. You're keen, I can tell. What about our working sisters?"

I didn't know what she meant at first, then I got it. I could talk to Lizzie and Annie and Gertie and Ivy and Ardis. Maybe the girls that worked in the wash house too, Bridie and Sally. And even Ina and Flora. It was never too soon to start.

"We should have our own march," I said. "We could march around Harrison Hot Springs."

"Brilliant!" said Abigail.

Chapter Seven

Lizzie spent the afternoon curled up on her bed with the worst case of cramps from her monthlies that I'd ever seen.

When I had a few spare minutes, I dashed outside and foraged for dandelion leaves in the rough grass behind the kitchen garden. The gardener, Mr. Bains, was nowhere in sight, but in the middle of the vegetables a boy was hoeing between rows of lettuce. I'd seen him with the bellboys and I knew his name was Mop. It was easy to see why – he had a mass of wild black curls.

He stopped hoeing and called out, "What are you looking for?"

I yelled back, "Dandelions!"

He scratched his head. "What for?"

"Nothing important." I could hardly tell him about Lizzie's monthlies.

"Can I help you?"

"No, thank you."

I spotted a patch of young bright green dandelions and got down on my hands and knees. As I carefully picked the tender leaves and laid them in my basket, I thought about Aunt Ginny. How many times had we done this very thing together?

A pair of black muddy boots planted themselves beside me. I looked up.

Mop grinned. "Are you making soup?"

"No."

"I know. Salad."

"No."

He gave an exaggerated sigh. "I give up."

I felt at a distinct disadvantage, squatting on the ground while he loomed over me. With as much dignity as I could muster, I stood up.

He tilted his head. "You've got dirt on your nose."

Honestly. I ignored him, snatched a generous sprig of parsley from beside the pea bed and marched back inside.

Glenys was alone in the kitchen, trimming asparagus. I chopped the dandelion leaves into small pieces and put them in a brown teapot with some parsley. I poured boiling water over top from the kettle on the stove and waited for the tea to steep.

I glanced up once. Glenys was watching me, her mouth partly open.

"For Lizzie," I said. "She's got awful cramps."

Glenys flushed. "I'm sure it's none of my business."

I put the teapot and a cup on a tray and left.

⁓

"I feel better already," said Lizzie. "I really do." She was sitting up, sipping the scalding tea. "Imagine you knowing about dandelion and parsley tea for cramps."

"It's because of Aunt Ginny. She's always making strange teas and tinctures, and people come from all over Victoria to buy them. She spends half her time in ditches hunting for plants and there's always something brewing on her stove."

Lizzie took another sip and made a face. "It tastes horrible."

"That's why it works. You think that's bad. Wait till you get a headache. I've got a remedy for that too."

"Spare me. Tell me again about Abigail and our march. When are we going to make the posters?"

"Tonight. Tell everyone who wants to help. I'll pinch some of the hotel stationery when Mrs. Bannerman's not looking. And I'll borrow some pens and ink wells from the library."

∾

Five of us met in our room: me, Lizzie, Ardis, Rachel and Gertie.

"Poor Annie," said Ardis, as I passed around paper, pens and bottles of ink. "She wanted ever so much to help. She says because she lives at home she never gets to do the fun things."

"She's coming to the march," I said. "Now, we need to decide what day."

"Saturday," said Lizzie. "There's always a quiet time in the afternoon. It's the best time for us to sneak out."

"Two o'clock," I said.

"What are we going to call ourselves?" said Rachel.

"Harrison Hot Springs Women's Freedom League." It gave me goosebumps just to say it.

"That's a lot to print," sighed Gertie. "And my letters always go crooked."

"It's perfect," said Lizzie.

We had finished fifteen posters when there was a knock on the door. Everyone froze.

Lizzie opened the door a crack. "It's just Effie. Come on in, Ef."

Effie stared at the posters. "You'll get into so much trouble with Mrs. Bannerman."

"She won't find out," I said.

"Now what?" said Ardis.

"We'll hand out the posters to all the maids and ask them to pass them around," I said.

Lizzie gathered up the pens. "But they can't show them to anyone else."

"We can put one in the staff dining room," said Ardis.

I shook my head. "Too risky."

"Where are we going to meet?" said Rachel.

Lizzie and I looked at each other. "Behind the hotel at the pavilion," said Lizzie. "I still can't believe we're doing this!"

"A banner," I said. "We need a banner. And I'll ask Abigail to make a speech. Something inspiring!"

Chapter Eight

"It's time to take up Mr. Doyle's eggs and toast," said Mrs. Wiggs. "He's asked for you to bring the tray, Charlotte. I dare say I'm surprised. He must have taken a shine to you."

When I got to his room, Effie was leaving with an armful of crumpled towels.

Mr. Doyle was in an armchair, reading a newspaper. "Set the tray here, there's a good girl." He cleared some writing paper from a small table. "I think I frightened that poor little maid. She crept in like a mouse and I was still in bed. I rose up out of the blankets like some great big growly bear and now she won't say a word to me."

I laughed. "That's just Effie. She's afraid of everyone. She practically faints if Mrs. Bannerman even looks at her."

I poured his tea. "Is there anything else you need?"

"Information. Those four lovely ladies who travel together. Have you seen them up and about this morning?"

"You mean the widows. They set out an hour ago on a lake excursion."

Mr. Doyle smiled. "Ah. The coast is clear. I can venture down now."

"Colonel Mitterand is downstairs in the lobby," I said. "He's asking people to join him in the bar."

The smile left his face. "Mitterand."

I remembered Mr. Doyle's words on the verandah when he saw Colonel Mitterand. *Damn you*, he'd muttered, not loud enough for

Colonel Mitterand to hear. They didn't like each other. Why?

"He's a bloody gossip. Excuse me, Charlotte, I shouldn't have said that. At any rate, I'll stay here for a while."

I turned to go. A chess board was set up on a second table that he had moved beside him, the pieces arranged as if a game had been interrupted. I didn't stop to think. I moved the black knight three spaces.

"That's an odd move," said Mr. Doyle.

"Not really." I showed him how the moves would go from there – the white rook, the black bishop, the white queen. "Checkmate!" I said.

"Not only do you play chess," said Mr. Doyle, "you play extremely well."

"I shouldn't have done that. I've ruined your game. Whoever you're playing with is going to be cross."

"I play by myself. I set up the board and then imagine how I would get out of a tricky situation. Tell me. Where did you learn to play?"

"From my father. I was only six. When we finished our game, he let me play with the pieces on the floor. I had great battles! And I play all the time with Mr. Chang. He's my aunt's boarder. He's also taught me how to play mahjong."

"I often watch some gentlemen playing mahjong in Beacon Hill Park. It looks very challenging."

"It is. Mr. Chang is a master but I'm not very good yet."

"I'm sure you'll be a formidable opponent one day. How old are you, Charlotte?"

"Almost sixteen. My birthday is on Empire Day weekend."

"That's just two weeks away. Were you raised in Harrison Hot Springs?"

"Oh no, sir. Toronto. But I live in Victoria now."

"You're so far away from your parents. You'll miss them."

"I live with my aunt. My parents died when I was ten."

"I'm so sorry to hear that."

I headed back downstairs to the kitchen.

If only all the guests were as nice as Mr. Doyle.

∾

"There. Done." Lizzie closed her book.

I set my cuffs and collar on the hot water radiator to dry. "Are you finally writing about me?"

"You're not that interesting, my dear." Lizzie yawned. "Long day. And by the way, Annie said Mop was asking about you. He works in the garden with Mr. Bains."

"I know."

"He's awfully nice, Char."

I remembered the dandelions. "And annoying."

"I think he's handsome. And all the girls like him. Ivy's been trying to get him to notice her for months."

I pulled a stocking out of my sewing basket and sat on my bed, searching for the hole. "I plan to be a suffragette."

"That doesn't mean you can't have a boyfriend. You don't want to end up like the receptionist, Miss Sweet. She's a spinster and has to keep house for her doddering old parents in Agassiz."

"Aunt Ginny's a spinster. And she's happy."

"Who's happy?" said Beatrice, pushing open the door.

"No one." I tossed my stocking back in the basket. It could wait 'til tomorrow.

Beatrice flopped on her cot. "You do this every time. *Every* time. As soon as I come in here, you stop talking. Like you have all these secrets and I'm not supposed to know."

"Mrs. Bannerman's happy," I said.

Beatrice blinked at me. "What?"

Lizzie laughed. "Hurry and get changed, Beatrice. We're blowing out the candles in five minutes!"

Chapter Nine

"Mrs. Bannerman wants to see you in her office," said Gertie. "Now."

Lizzie and I were folding napkins in the dining room.

"She's found out about the march!" I said.

"I'll go with you," said Lizzie.

"Better not. I'll be right back." I sounded braver than I felt.

Mrs. Bannerman stared at me across her desk. "What have you been saying to Mr. Doyle?"

"Me? Nothing?"

"He wants you to play chess with him this afternoon."

My mouth fell open.

"I don't know what he's thinking of," said Mrs. Bannerman. "I've never heard of such a thing. He went to Mr. Brown instead of me. I'd have made short work of this nonsense." Her eyes narrowed. "I'd like to know your part in this, Charlotte."

"I didn't do anything wrong."

"Why do I find that hard to believe? Mr. Doyle is expecting you at two o'clock. Don't be late. You'll use the upstairs parlour. You may go back to your duties now."

I knew how Mrs. Bannerman's mind worked. There would be fewer guests upstairs to see us. I hurried back to the dining room to tell Lizzie.

⁓

Mr. Doyle put his hand over the white bishop and then took it away. "I just don't know...I have to think about this a little longer."

He was taking forever with every move. I had a hundred things to do before dinner.

He picked up the white rook and moved it four squares.

I studied the board and slid the black rook three squares. "Check!"

Mr. Doyle tried to save himself with his knight.

I moved in my queen. "Checkmate!"

"I didn't see that coming!" said Mr. Doyle.

"It's Mr. Chang's favourite move."

I stood up. It was my turn to fill the salt and pepper shakers. And I still had all the silver teapots to polish.

"You must stay. I asked Mrs. Bannerman to send tea up at three o'clock." Mr. Doyle took his watch out of his waistcoat pocket. "It should be here any minute."

I sank back on my chair. Mrs. Bannerman would kill me.

Annie brought in a tray laden with tea and slices of pound cake. She made funny faces behind Mr. Doyle's back. I bit my cheeks to keep from laughing.

My worries rushed back and I gulped my tea.

Mr. Doyle stirred two sugar lumps into his cup. "Tell me about this march you're planning."

I spilled tea on my apron. "You know about it?"

"I saw one of your posters."

"Where? It's supposed to be a secret."

"Someone left it on a bench by the lake."

"You mustn't tell Mrs. Bannerman!"

Mr. Doyle looked solemn. "I won't."

I glanced at the door and lowered my voice. "Annie's mother is making us a banner. It's red flannel with black silk letters. HHSWFL. It stands for Harrison Hot Springs Women's Freedom League."

"A brilliant name!"

"I thought of it myself."

"I'm not surprised. I'd love to hear more but you'd better go. I don't want you getting into trouble. We'll give Mrs. Bannerman time to cool down and we'll have another game."

Mrs. Bannerman was marching up the stairs as I made my way down. "Do you have any idea how long you've been, young lady?"

I tried to sidle past.

"Your job is serving tables," she said. "Not having tea with the guests and pretending you're a lady."

～

After dinner in the staff dining room, Clarence leaped onto a chair. He waved a poster above his head. "Votes for Women!"

"How did you get that?" I said.

"What is it?" said Beatrice. "What does it say?"

I jumped up and tried to grab Clarence's arm. "Rachel! Help me!"

Rachel pushed back her chair. A jug of water tipped over, flooding the table.

"Rach! Careful!" Ivy grabbed a napkin and tried to sop up the water streaming into her lap.

"Never trust a woman wearing trousers!" yelled Fred.

"It's about that suffragette, isn't it?" said Beatrice. "I think it's really strange the way she dresses. You'd never catch *me* in trousers! Yesterday I heard –"

"Clarence, give it back!" said Gertie.

Clarence's chair tipped over. He fell, crashing into Mike. They sprawled across the floor, laughing.

Beatrice screamed.

"Shut up, you little fool," said Fred. "You'll have Bannerman in here."

I grabbed the poster.

"Run, Charlotte!" said Gertie.

Chapter Ten

When I took Mr. Doyle his breakfast the next morning, he was at a
table by the window writing a postcard. It was one of the postcards
that Miss Sweet sold at the front desk, with a picture of the St. Alice
on the front and the words *Finest health and pleasure resort in America.*
Vapour and private baths.

His hand holding the pen was still. He pushed the postcard to the
side. I saw the words *My dear Henry* written with a flourish. The rest
of the postcard was blank.

"Did you enjoy your dinner last night?" I said. Dr. Herman had
invited Mr. Doyle to dinner at his house in the village. I'd seen him
leaving, wearing a top hat and carrying an overcoat over his arm.

"I had a superb time. Mrs. Herman is an outstanding cook. And Dr.
Herman is a most interesting man. He has a collection of curios from
all over the world. He is especially fond of India. He is off tomorrow
to Vancouver to consult on a case of shingles. He's an expert on the
condition."

He reached for his jar of marmalade. I left him happily buried in
a newspaper.

~~~

I returned to Mr. Doyle's room before lunch to collect his tray. He was
on the verandah having coffee with Mr. Timmins.

I had keys but, as usual, his door was unlocked. He'd stacked his
dishes on the tray and wiped up his crumbs.

I gathered up his napkin. Underneath was the postcard, ripped into two pieces. I picked up the pieces and held them together.

Dear Henry,

I deeply regret

Nothing more.

"I've come back for my newspaper," said Mr. Doyle.

I spun around, dropping the pieces of postcard. "I'm so sorry...I didn't mean –"

"I write to Henry every day. But I never seem to get very far."

"Is he your son?"

"No. He calls me Uncle Jacob but he's not my real nephew. His mother Fanny was a dear friend. She was an actress."

"That sounds glamorous."

"She was very glamorous, indeed. And a wonderful mother. When Henry was a little boy, Fanny used to take him to Beacon Hill Park to sail his toy boat on the pond. One day his boat escaped and I rescued it. We became great chums."

Mr. Doyle seemed to want to talk about Henry. I didn't feel bad for snooping any longer. "What kinds of things did you do together?"

"We'd go to the cricket matches and for rides in my motor car and I taught him to row. I've watched him grow up into a fine young man."

"Doesn't he have a father?"

"His father died when he was a baby. Fanny died five months ago. I'm really the only person he has but he –"

Mr. Doyle fell silent.

"That's so sad," I said.

"Yes, it is."

Mr. Doyle picked up his newspaper.

I walked back to the kitchen, lost in thought about Henry.

What did Mr. Doyle deeply regret?

Chapter Eleven

Mr. Doyle spread marmalade on his toast. "Have you picked the route for the march?"

"Right down the village street and back to the St. Alice. Abigail is going to make a speech in front of *Inkman's*. It has to be short because we don't dare be away for more than an hour."

"Your parents would have been proud of you."

I hesitated.

"Would you like to see their photograph?"

"I would."

I dashed past Mrs. Bannerman's closed door and raced up the stairs, two at a time, to fetch my photograph.

"It's a little blurry," I said. "I think they moved. Their names were Arthur and Katherine O'Dell."

Mr. Doyle studied the photograph for a long time.

"I don't look at all like my mother," I said. "She had such wonderful hair."

He smiled. "Katherine. Katie."

"That's what everyone called her! How did you know?"

"Just a guess."

He handed the photograph back to me. "She's beautiful."

⌒⌒

After the guests had gone to bed, Abigail slipped up the back stairs to our room. Everyone except Beatrice and Glenys crowded in: Ardis,

42

Gertie, Rachel, the girls from the wash house, Sally and Bridie, Effie and Ivy. Three to a bed, the rest sitting on the floor. Annie had gone home. I vowed to memorize every detail to tell her.

Abigail perched on the end of my bed, cross-legged like a man.

"Imagine. Three thousand women marching to Exeter Hall. It was called the Mud March. I was staying in London with my aunt and Papa had forbidden me to go. He said it would turn into a riot. But I went anyway."

"Why was it called the Mud March?" said Rachel.

"It was pouring down rain and the streets were clogged with mud. I waited until my aunt dozed off and then I ran miles in my galoshes. You should have seen me. Splattered in mud from head to toe."

"Then what happened?" said Ivy.

"I heard the band in the distance and then the procession was right in front of me. I jumped in. It was like boarding an express train."

"Brave you," said Gertie.

"You'd have done it too. We're sisters in the cause! I wish I could describe it better. Everyone waving banners and signs and shouting *Deeds Not Words!* And a whole lot of carriages and motor cars blaring their horns and bringing up the rear. We made history that day." Her hands clenched into fists. "I have to convince Papa to let me come home. There's another march next month at Hyde Park."

"Deeds not words!" I cried.

"Votes for women!" said Lizzie.

"Shhh," said Effie. "Mrs. Bannerman."

"Now we'll go around the room and everyone will say what they want to do with their life," said Abigail. "I'll go first. I'm going to be a journalist."

"A pharmacist," I said.

"An author," said Lizzie.

Ardis dreamed of being a teacher, Gertie a nurse, Ivy a dress shop owner. "I'm going to be a florist," said Sally. I looked at her poor hands, chapped and red from washing sheets all day.

"I don't know," wailed Bridie.

"That's fine," said Abigail. "As long as you're thinking about it."

"I want to be married," whispered Effie. "I'm sorry. I just do."

Abigail patted Effie's arm. "We're not *against* men. We're *for* women's rights. But you must make sure, Effie, that your husband doesn't treat you like a servant."

Deeds not words. If I wanted to be a pharmacist, I'd have to go back to school. I'd heard they were looking for waitresses at the brand new Empress Hotel. I could work in the evenings and weekends. My head buzzed with plans.

Chapter Twelve

Lizzie passed me in the swinging doorway, carrying a tray of bowls of Cream of Wheat. "Glenys is giving hints to Mrs. Wiggs about the march. We've got to stop her."

"How did she find out?"

"Don't know."

I set my empty coffee pot on the kitchen table, just in time to hear Glenys say, "I think a woman's place is in the home. Don't you, Mrs. Wiggs?"

"There's a place for working women, too," said Mrs. Wiggs. "As we both know, Glenys."

I thought quickly. "Mrs. Wiggs, could we discuss the lunch menu?" Mrs. Wiggs stared at me.

"It's silly for women to want the vote," persisted Glenys.

"I don't know what you're nattering on about." Mrs. Wiggs slid a pan of sizzling sausages onto a platter. "Mr. Wiggs says a woman would do a better job of running this country than a man. I dare say she would."

"I just don't think, on a busy Saturday, people should be making other plans," said Glenys.

"Come on, girls," said Mrs. Wiggs. "These sausages are getting cold."

∽∾

By mid morning, the drizzle had stopped and the sun was trying to shine. I carried cups of coffee out to the verandah. Mr. Doyle, Mrs. Webster, Abigail and Mrs. Chisholm were sitting together.

"English marmalade!" said Abigail. "It's far superior."

"Now there, young lady," said Mr. Doyle. "That's where you are mistaken. No one can beat the Scottish for marmalade."

"He brings a supply every year," said Mrs. Webster. "He keeps it hidden in his room and refuses to share."

Mr. Doyle turned to Mrs. Chisholm. "Miranda, you must come to my defense."

"I much prefer strawberry jam," said Mrs. Chisholm.

As I walked away, Mr. Doyle roared with laughter.

∞

One by one, we slipped out the back door and raced across the grass to meet Abigail at the pavilion. Me, Lizzie, Annie, Gertie, Ardis, Rachel, Ivy, Sally, Ina and Flora. In all, there were fourteen of us. Even Abigail's sister, Sarah, was there, smiling. "A new recruit," Abigail whispered to me. I tried not to think of the abandoned guests.

"Line up, everyone," said Abigail. "We'll go side by side in pairs. Annie and Rachel, you go at the front and carry the banner. Charlotte, you bring up the rear. Keep Ina and Flora in front of you so you can watch them."

At the last second, Mop stepped into the space beside me.

"What are *you* doing here?" I said.

"I want to be part of it."

Abigail, who was striding up and down the line like a mother duck herding her ducklings, said, "Welcome! If anything's going to change, we need men on our side. Now listen, everyone. We can't make any noise until we get off the hotel grounds."

"There's a path from here that will take us right out to the road to the village," said Lizzie. "We can start the march there."

Abigail had told us to bring anything we could find to wave in the air. We had a dazzling collection of hankies, scarfs and even an embroidered pillow case.

"Deeds not Words! Votes for Women!" Our voices rang as we marched along the road.

A crowd of spectators, mostly guests from the hotel who were out walking, fell in step beside us.

The tennis players were sitting by the lake, eating ice creams. "How hilarious!" cried the girl with long blond hair. All four of them jumped up and joined our parade.

We were halfway to *Inkman's* when I heard a *beep beep* behind us. It was Mr. Timmins in his motor car with Mr. Doyle beside him, waving a bright red handkerchief.

A group of loggers reeled down the road toward us. "Hello, darlings! Give a man a kiss!"

A woman in a print dress came out of the front door of Dr. Herman's house and waved. "Good for you, girls!"

When we got to *Inkman's*, Miss Sweet was coming out with a shopping bag. Her mouth dropped open. Mr. Inkman stood in the doorway behind her. "You're welcome to be here but not inside the store," he said.

"Speech! Speech!" we all shouted.

Abigail leaped up on a bench. I drank in every word.

"We've been oppressed too long...our sisters in London are behind us...we WILL get the vote!"

When we finally started back, we were a huge noisy crowd.

"Look!" said Lizzie. "Miss Sweet's marching too!"

We lost all track of time. We forgot everything except the march.

At the bend in the road stood Mrs. Bannerman.

Chapter Thirteen

"Disgraceful." Mrs. Bannerman leaned across her desk. "Shameful. Reprehensible."

An hour ago, we had been blazing a new path for women's rights. Now we were defending ourselves to a livid Mrs. Bannerman.

She turned on Lizzie. "Elizabeth! Whatever possessed you?"

"It was my idea," I blurted out. There was no way I was going to let Lizzie take the blame.

"I'm part of it, too," said Lizzie.

"Women should have the vote," I declared. "I read about it in a...a magazine." I couldn't tell Mrs. Bannerman that the idea for the march came from Abigail. No fraternizing with the guests was her strictest rule.

I was breaking rules right and left. What made me move the pieces on Mr. Doyle's chess board? Plunk down on the bench to talk to Abigail? Encourage the maids to go behind Mrs. Bannerman's back?

She was going to sack me for sure.

"Charlotte, you leave me no choice –"

I braced myself.

"The guests loved it," piped up Ardis.

"That's right," said Annie. "They followed us and cheered and Mr. Timmins honked his horn."

"Mr. Doyle said it's the most fun he's had for years," said Lizzie.

"Two days wages," said Mrs. Bannerman. "Now back to work. All of you."

I still had my job. Checkmate.

~

"I'll talk to Mrs. Bannerman," said Abigail. "I insist. She's a woman. She'll listen to reason."

Lizzie, Annie and I waited down the hall from Mrs. Bannerman's office.

In less than five minutes, Abigail burst back through the door. "I'm so mad I could spit! She's a traitor to the cause. I feel so terrible about your wages. She wouldn't budge."

"It was worth it," said Lizzie.

"I'd do it again," said Annie.

"Did you hear about Miss Sweet?" I said. "She told Mr. Brown he'd get the list of new guests when she was good and ready."

~

Lizzie straightened her apron in front of the mirror while I laced up my boots. "Where are you going in such a hurry? It's your afternoon off."

"If you must know, Mop and I are going up the mountain."

"Well done," said Lizzie.

"I'm not interested in –"

"Have fun."

I picked up my basket and shut the door firmly behind me. Mop was waiting on the path to the Bath House.

"What do you think of the decorations?" he said.

The boys and Mr. Bains had been getting ready all week for Empire Day. They'd wrapped red, white and blue ribbons around the pillars. Pots of red petunias glowed in the sun. A Union Jack hung from each end of the verandah.

"Beautiful."

"We've got fireworks. Shooting stars and rockets and those huge balls that look like they're exploding. Mr. Bains put me in charge."

The trail up the mountain started at the Bath House. It was steep and we puffed too much to talk. It finally levelled off in an open sunny patch with a magnificent view of the lake below us.

I gazed around. "Wild violets! They're everywhere!"

I knelt down and picked tiny leaves and delicate purple flowers and placed them in my basket.

"What are those for?" said Mop.

"Violets steeped in milk do wonders for the complexion." I was planning an evening of pampering for Lizzie and me.

Mop raised his eyebrows. "Maybe I should try some. How do you *know* stuff like that?"

"Aunt Ginny." I told him about her tinctures and medicines. "One day, I'm going to be a pharmacist."

"A pharmacist. Impressive. And I bet you'll do it too. Deeds not words, right? And let me guess. Those dandelions you picked were to cure warts."

"You'll never know. What about you? Are you going to stay at the St. Alice forever?"

"Not a chance." He flopped down on the grass beside me. "I'm gaining experience. A family called the Butcharts are building an amazing garden at Tod Inlet near Victoria. They've already finished the Japanese garden and they have plans for a sunken garden. It's going to be a showcase. You wait and see. One day, I'm going to be the head gardener."

Mop leaned over and removed a piece of grass from my hair.

We stared at each other.

"May I kiss you?" he said.

I had never been kissed before. I felt my face turn crimson.

"Sorry. Misunderstood," he said.

We scrambled down the mountain in silence. I tried not to brush against him. On the steep part at the end, I stumbled and almost fell. Mop caught my arm but as soon as we reached the path to the hotel, his hand dropped away.

Chapter Fourteen

Mr. Doyle and Mr. Timmins dined together at a quiet table in the corner.

"I'll have the marinated avocados for starters, followed by lobster bisque and salmon poached in butter sauce," said Mr. Timmins.

"Lobster bisque." Mr. Doyle shuddered. "Can you get me a cup of consommé, Charlotte? And see if it's possible to have the salmon poached in a clear broth. I can't face butter sauce tonight."

I carried the tray of soups into the dining room. "I managed to get the consommé but Mr. Pincer says you'll have to scrape the sauce off the fish."

When I collected their soup bowls, Mr. Doyle had barely touched his consommé. "Something must have disagreed with me at lunch. I don't understand it. I had the same thing as you, old chap. Tomato salad and a veal cutlet."

"Perhaps the veal was off," said Mr. Timmins.

"You'd better not let Mrs. Wiggs hear you. And besides, you feel fine."

"It's very odd."

Mr. Doyle stood up. "I'm abandoning you, I'm afraid. I'm going to lie down."

"But you'll miss dessert!" I cried. "It's lemon tarts!"

Mr. Doyle groaned. "God forbid. Be a good girl, Charlotte, and bring me some tea to my room."

∼✿∼

I collected a handful of mint leaves in Mr. Bains's garden.

Mr. Pincer had gone back to his cottage and Glenys was alone in the kitchen. She was kneading bread dough on a wooden board and setting it in pans for dinner rolls for tomorrow. I nodded at her and took the leaves over to the sink.

I filled the kettle and set it on the big black range to boil. I washed the mint leaves and listened to the thump thump thump of Glenys's big hands.

I lifted a small brown teapot off a shelf. I put the leaves in the bottom of the teapot and filled it with steaming water.

I could feel Glenys watching me. "Making tea out of old leaves again?" she said.

"It's for Mr. Doyle."

Glenys punched the mound of dough. "It don't seem right to me."

✴

Mr. Doyle took a long sip of the peppermint tea. "This will do the trick."

"You don't look well," I said.

"I've a dreadful headache," he admitted. "And my eyes are giving me problems today."

"Don't you think you should call Dr. Herman?"

Mr. Doyle rubbed his temple. "He's away in Vancouver consulting on a case."

"There must be another doctor. You could get some powders or something."

"There's Dr. Markham in Chilliwack but I don't want to bother him to come all this way. When I was in South Africa, I picked up a case of malaria. It sometimes comes back to haunt me. This must be what this is."

"Malaria! That sounds frightening."

"That's the trouble with this blasted disease," said Mr. Doyle. "It never completely goes away. Never mind, I'll be back to my old self soon. Ready to take you on again in another game of chess."

~∞~

Just before dinner the next day, Mrs. Bannerman called me into her office. She was holding a yellow envelope. "It's a telegram for you. Frank picked it up on his afternoon run to Agassiz." She frowned. "It's not usual for our chauffeur to be delivering telegrams to the maids."

"No, Ma'am." I wanted to grab the envelope from her hand. Who was sending me a telegram?

"You'd better read it here," said Mrs. Bannerman.

She handed me the envelope. I opened it and took out a thin piece of paper. "It's from Mr. Chang." It was short, just four words. I read it out loud. "Aunt Ginny is missing."

"Who is this Mr. Chang?" said Mrs. Bannerman.

"My aunt's boarder. She used to run a boarding house and he's the last one left."

"I see. Does your aunt do this often? Go missing?"

"Never. I've got to go home."

"Absolutely not. It's Empire Day weekend. By tomorrow afternoon, the hotel will be full."

"I've got to. She's my only family."

"And I have a hotel to run."

We stared at each other.

"Please." I was going anyway. Nothing could stop me.

"This is most inconvenient."

Mrs. Bannerman tapped her finger on her desk. "I suppose I could move Rachel into the dining room. Very well. I'll grant you this leave. You can go on the omnibus in the morning to the train station. You must be back by Tuesday at the very latest. If you aren't, I shall have to let you go."

∽

Mr. Doyle didn't come to dinner. When the last tables were cleared and the fresh cloths and cutlery set out for morning, I went upstairs to tell him about Aunt Ginny.

"Oh, Charlotte, that's such a worry," he said.

"I don't know what it means, that she's missing. She could have had a terrible accident and be lying in a hospital. Anything could have happened!"

"You must let me know if there's anything I can do to help."

I spotted an envelope lying on his table. The name on the front was Henry.

For a moment, I forgot my troubles. "Mr. Doyle! You've written to Henry!"

"Yes. It's going to his boarding school in Victoria." He hesitated. "I hate to ask you when you've got so much on your mind. The mail is so slow from here. Is there any chance you could drop it in a postbox in Victoria?"

"Of course." I tucked it into my apron.

Mr. Doyle sighed.

"I fear Henry will tear it up but I have to try."

VICTORIA

1908

Chapter Fifteen

Mrs. Wiggs had packed me some ham sandwiches but I only nib-
bled at the corners. By the time *The Princess Royal* docked in Victoria
Harbour, my stomach was twisted into knots. The cries of seagulls
and the smells of salty fish, seaweed and black tar swirled around me.

I left the dock and hurried past the grey stone Parliament Buildings
and the enormous Empress Hotel. Horse-drawn carriages and a few
motor cars thronged the streets.

I stopped several times and set my suitcase down and rested. It was
dusk when I reached the quiet country lane near Beacon Hill Park.

Aunt Ginny's tall narrow house was called Buttercup House but
the bright yellow paint had faded to a pale peeling mustard.

Mr. Chang was on the front porch, in his usual chair, reading a
Chinese newspaper. Beside him, in one of her lumpy hand knitted
sweaters, her grey hair falling out of its pins, was Aunt Ginny.

"What happened?" I cried. "Are you all right?"

"I'm fine," said Aunt Ginny.

"Where were you?"

"Right here."

I dropped my suitcase with a thump. "You tricked me! I could have lost my job because of you! And you scared me to death."

"Don't be silly. You're not spending your sixteenth birthday in some hotel on the other side of the ocean."

I sighed. Aunt Ginny had never left Vancouver Island and the mainland was as distant to her as Japan.

"Mr. Chang, I can't believe you wrote that telegram. How did she persuade you?"

"It wasn't easy," admitted Aunt Ginny.

Mr. Chang raised his hands. "What could I do?"

"I'm going back to the St. Alice tomorrow."

"You can't," said Aunt Ginny. "I've baked you a birthday cake."

"I should have known I can't trust you. How many times did you come to my school with stories of doctor appointments and instead we ended up in a ditch picking herbs?"

"Charlotte dear, that reminds me. I want you to run an errand for me tomorrow morning."

She wiped her gnarled hands on her apron. "I need some fresh ginseng root and a few other herbs from Sing Lee."

Aunt Ginny was hopeless.

"And then," she said, "in the afternoon we'll have your cake and presents."

ᴈᴧᴄ

I put Aunt Ginny's list (*white mustard seed, mulberry bark, tiger's bone, ginseng root*) and Henry's letter in my bag. I took my bicycle out of the shed at the bottom of the garden. Aunt Ginny had found it abandoned at Beacon Hill Park, and it was the only mechanical thing she approved of. I went everywhere on it and had named it Rosemary.

I put my bag in the wire basket, jumped on Rosemary and pedaled down the dusty streets to the gates of Chinatown. I ventured into Fan Tan Alley, wheeling my bicycle past an opium factory and a laundry where a man with a pigtail stirred clothes in a huge steaming vat. The air smelled of cooking meat, burning joss sticks and wet bamboo. I left Rosemary outside the door of Sing Lee's shop and took my bag inside.

A bell tinkled over the door. Sing Lee looked up from a parcel he was wrapping in brown paper. "No auntie today?"

I smiled and shook my head and passed him the list. While Sing Lee was assembling the herbs, measuring carefully on an old tarnished scale, I looked at the rows of bottles, some dusty, on the shelves behind him. Sing Lee made medicines and occasionally Aunt Ginny had purchased a bottle for stomach ailments or fever.

I had a sudden thought. "Do you have anything for malaria?"

"Malaria. Great sickness in Africa."

"Yes."

He reached for a blue bottle with a label with Chinese characters on it.

I felt a flash of excitement. "How much?"

He scribbled a sum on a piece of paper. I handed him the coins. He wrapped the bottle and I put it in my bag with my other purchases. As I left the shop, I prayed that Sing Lee's medicine would help Mr. Doyle. I stowed my bag in Rosemary's basket and pulled out the envelope for Henry.

St Bartholomew's School for Boys.

I had cycled past there lots of times. More than anything, I wanted to meet Henry. I jumped on my bicycle.

Chapter Sixteen

I cycled through an open iron gate and up a long driveway, shaded with leafy maple trees. *Saint Bartholomew's School for Boys* was a brick mansion with ivy-covered stone pillars. I leaned Rosemary against a pillar, took a deep breath and pushed open the heavy front door.

I stepped into a gloomy foyer with a scuffed wooden floor and a grand staircase. Straight ahead of me was a closed door with a sign that said *Receptionist.*

I stood there, listening to the sound of a clacking typewriter, and then knocked.

"Come in," said a voice.

A thin woman sitting at a desk looked up from the typewriter. "Yes?"

"I'm here to see Henry Carter."

"I'm afraid that's not possible."

"But I must see him. I've a letter from his uncle."

"Henry is at Corrig College playing cricket."

"May I wait 'til he gets back?"

"Most certainly not. You can leave the letter with me."

I dug it out of my bag and handed it to her. As I turned to go, shouts of laughter drifted through an open window.

Back in the foyer, boys in shorts and shirts with the sleeves rolled up crowded through the front door. Was one of them Henry?

I couldn't just stand there and stare. I went outside and retrieved Rosemary. I cycled as far as the iron gate. A gear clanked and my pedal jammed. I climbed off and surveyed the dangling chain. Not again!

Soon my hands were slippery with grease.

A boy coasted down the driveway on a bicycle that looked much newer than Rosemary. He skidded to a stop. "Trouble?"

I looked up. He had black hair, a long straight nose and dark blue eyes. "I can manage, thank you."

The chain pinched my finger.

"Ouch," he said. "I bet that hurt."

I frowned.

"I'm Henry Carter."

Henry! I hadn't expected him to be so good looking. "I'm Charlotte O'Dell."

"Are you the girl who brought me the letter?"

"Yes."

"How exactly did you get it?" he said.

"Mr. Doyle gave it to me at the St. Alice Hotel in Harrison Hot Springs."

"Right. The St. Alice. What were you doing there?"

"I work there."

"Really."

"I'm a waitress."

The chain jumped off its track again.

"So why are you in Victoria?"

"I'm just here for the weekend. Visiting."

"For Empire Day, I bet. Where are you staying?"

Why was my chain choosing now to be so stubborn? "At Buttercup House with my aunt. By Beacon Hill Park."

"You're getting grease on your dress."

"Yes, I can see that." I grabbed a stick and tried to lift up the sagging chain.

"There's an easier way," he said.

I bent my head down.

He slid back on his bicycle seat. He called over his shoulder, "I won't read it, you know. I won't even open it."

⚬⚬

As soon as Henry left, the chain slid smoothly into place.

I pedaled home with Aunt Ginny's herbs and roots. She was in the kitchen, spreading chocolate frosting on a tall cake. Mr. Chang sat at the table. In front of him were two small packages wrapped in brown paper and tied with red yarn. One was thin and flat and the other looked like a little box.

"You've been a long time, dear," said Aunt Ginny. "Mr. Chang's been waiting."

Mr. Chang winked at me. It was Aunt Ginny who adored birthdays. She made me the exact same cake every year. Suddenly I was glad I'd come back.

I washed my greasy hands in the sink with a bar of Aunt Ginny's yellow soap. Then I went into my tiny bedroom behind the kitchen. I put the bottle of malaria medicine in my suitcase and changed out of my greasy dress into a skirt and blouse.

Aunt Ginny cut slices of the dark rich cake. When the last crumb was gone, Mr. Chang proclaimed, "Delicious!"

"Now the presents," said Aunt Ginny. "Mr. Chang's first."

Mr. Chang handed me the thin flat package. I tore off the brown paper. It was a small pocket knife in a leather case.

"I hope it will be useful," he said.

"It's just what I need for Rosemary's stupid chain."

Next I unwrapped Aunt Ginny's gift. I lifted the lid of a little navy blue velvet box. A brooch nestled in a bed of cream silk. A robin with a sparkly red breast, a delicate black beak and a tiny black eye.

"Aunt Ginny!"

61

"Do you know where it came from?"

"It was Mama's!"

"Why don't you put it on?" said Mr. Chang.

Aunt Ginny pinned the brooch on my blouse. I ran into my bedroom and stood in front of my mirror. I remembered sitting beside Mama at her dressing table. The velvet box had been hidden at the back of her night table, and she had taken it out to show me.

"You can open it," Mama had said.

Breathlessly, I had picked up the little robin and cradled it in the palm of my hand. "Why don't you ever wear it?"

"Because I don't want your father to see it."

"Is it a secret?"

"Yes, it's our secret."

After that, Mama wore it, but only when my father was away.

And now it was mine.

I went back into the kitchen and hugged Aunt Ginny. "I never want to take it off."

Aunt Ginny's voice went gruff. "Mr. Chang, are you wanting another piece of cake?"

Chapter Seventeen

I left Aunt Ginny and Mr. Chang asleep in their chairs on the porch and I cycled along Dallas Road. The ocean was calm, the tide partly out. I smelled seaweed and salt.

I left Rosemary in a grassy field and hiked down a path to the rocky beach. I spotted Henry's bicycle, leaning against a log. I gazed down the beach. He was standing at the edge of the water, staring across at the mountains, his hands in his pockets. I hesitated. Then I picked my way across the slippery wet rocks. He turned, saw me and then looked back at the ocean.

"I think it's wrong that you won't read Mr. Doyle's letter," I said.

"Who said I wasn't going to read it?"

"You did."

"Right."

"He's been very ill."

Henry picked up a stone and sliced it across the water. He counted the bounces. "One, two, three, four."

Mr. Chang had taught me to skip stones. I searched for a smooth flat one. I flicked my wrist and sent it spinning. "One, two, three, four, *five.*"

A smile flickered across Henry's face. He reached into his pocket and took out a cigarette and matches.

He lit the cigarette. "Do you smoke?"

"No."

"Never tried?"

"Never."

"Do you want to?"

I had no intention of taking up smoking but I *was* a little curious. He passed me the cigarette. "Don't inhale."

I took a tiny little puff. I wrinkled my nose at the bitter taste and Henry laughed. I handed it back to him.

"My mother hated it when I started smoking," he said. "She said one day they'd discover that it was bad for you."

I remembered what Mr. Doyle had told me about Henry's mother. She was an actress called Fanny. They'd met over Henry's sailboat in Beacon Hill Park. She had died five months ago.

I bent down and turned over a rock, watching a tiny crab scuttle for shelter.

"So why do you live with your aunt?" said Henry.

I straightened up. "My parents are dead."

"Then we have something in common." He blew smoke into the still air. "We're both orphans."

He pulled the white envelope out of his other pocket. "He keeps bombarding me with postcards and letters and, I admit, I don't read them."

He stared at it and then tore it open and took out a single sheet of paper. I saw the letterhead: *The St. Alice Hotel Harrison Hot Springs*.

Mr. Doyle's flowing handwriting filled the page.

My dear boy...

I looked away.

Henry read in silence, "He signs it *your loving Uncle Jacob*. That's a lie." He crumpled up the letter.

"Why do you hate him so much?"

Henry dropped his cigarette on the beach and stepped on it. "It's complicated."

"Mr. Doyle said you were great chums."

"Did he? We *were*. I'll give him that much. My mother married again when I was twelve and I actually thought she was going to marry Uncle Jacob."

"But she didn't."

"No. Instead she married this jealous bastard Bernard Carter. She barely knew him."

"He sounds awful. How did they even meet?"

"He saw my mother in a play and then all of a sudden they were married and we were moving in with him and his mother." His face darkened. "Her name's Stella. She's a witch."

"He still lived with his mother?"

"Yes. Forty years old and he'd never left home. Stella has a house at the Gorge."

Two seagulls screeched, fighting over a dead fish. A black dog ran down the beach and barked. Henry pulled out another cigarette, stared at it and then put it back in his pocket.

"It's the last house on the Gorge road. My mother hated it there. It's so isolated. I hated it too. Mother married Carter on the condition that Uncle Jacob could stay in my life. Carter didn't like that but he had to agree. I would wait at the window watching for Uncle Jacob. I couldn't wait to get out of that house."

"You must have been so excited to go all those places with Mr. Doyle."

"Yes. And he arranged for me to go to boarding school. It's the best thing that ever happened to me. I've never been back to the Gorge since...well, since. Once school's over, I'll have to go back for a few days to sort through my mother's things. And then it's over."

"What are you going to do?"

"Don't know. I've been accepted to Queens but I'm not taking any more money from Uncle Jacob. He pays for *Saint Bartholomew's* but that's enough." He shrugged. "I'll survive."

"Could you at least write a reply?"

"No."

We walked back along the beach to his bicycle, leaning against the log. He wheeled it up the path to the road. "I can't believe I've told you all this. It's talking about Uncle Jacob. It brings it all back. Sorry about that. The last thing you want to hear is the depressing story of my life."

He watched me pick up Rosemary and gave me a half smile. "Chain working?"

"Perfectly."

"Well then, it was interesting meeting you, Charlotte O'Dell." He mounted his bike and sped away.

I thought he might turn around and wave, but he didn't.

Henry hadn't told me the whole story of his life. I still didn't know why he hated Mr. Doyle. And he hadn't told me how his mother Fanny had died.

I was sure something terrible had happened at the house at the Gorge.

Chapter Eighteen

In the morning, Aunt Ginny and I walked to St. Stephen's Church for the nine o'clock service. When we got back to Buttercup House, sitting on the top step of the porch was Henry, eating chocolate cake and talking to Mr. Chang.

He jumped up. "You must be Charlotte's aunt. I'm Henry. I'm pleased to meet you. And the cake is excellent. Charlotte kept her birthday a secret."

"Charlotte likes to be mysterious," said Aunt Ginny. "She's just like me."

I smiled. "Not exactly."

Henry was the last person I expected to see. "How did you find me?"

"Easy. You told me you lived at Buttercup House near Beacon Hill Park. I used all my fine detective skills. What are you doing now?"

Did I want to go with Henry? I'd been planning to take flowers to the cemetery but I had all afternoon. And I still wanted to find out what had happened between him and Mr. Doyle. "Unless Aunt Ginny needs me, nothing."

"You go and enjoy your day, dear," said Aunt Ginny.

"I'll get Rosemary," I said. "That's what I call my bicycle."

As we cycled along Dallas Road, Henry insisted we think of a name for his bicycle.

"Ebenezer?" he said.

"Too stuffy."

"George?"

"Too ordinary."

I pedaled faster, spurting ahead.

He puffed as he caught up to me. "I've got it. Pearl."

"That's a girl's name."

"Why can't my bicycle be a girl?"

"Because you're a boy?"

"But I like girls," said Henry.

⁓

We rode down Government Street and stopped for tea and sandwiches in the Dickens Café.

Between bites, Henry listed the scores of cricket matches and all the places his team travelled. "I'm the captain. It's the thing I'll miss most about *St. Bartholomew's.*"

He stared at the empty sandwich plate and then signaled to the waitress, who was lounging against the wall, looking like her feet ached. I knew all about that!

"So what's it like to be a waitress at the St. Alice?"

Hoping to make my life sound interesting, I described the lake and the steaming pools at the Bath House and the ride on the omnibus. I told him stories of Mr. Paisley and the Howards and Mrs. Bannerman.

"The bill," Henry said to the waitress.

I'd been going on quite a bit, saving our march to the end.

He listened, picking up crumbs with his fingers.

"I can just picture it. No one takes suffragettes seriously. That Abigail sounds like a horror in her trousers."

He glanced at the bill and pulled some coins out of his pocket.

"You don't know her," I said. "Thank you for the tea. I'm going to go now. I want to pick some flowers and take them to the cemetery."

"You have to do that now?"

"I want to. Everything's going to be so busy tomorrow with Empire Day. And then I leave really early on Tuesday morning."

"Is this for your parents' grave?"

"Not a grave. They're buried in Toronto. Aunt Ginny put a headstone in the Ross Bay Cemetery so I'd have somewhere to go and think about them."

"Is this a private thing you do?"

"Not exactly."

"Then I'll come too."

~~~

We found beautiful blue bachelor's buttons growing along the side of the road. I picked a bouquet while Henry leaned against the bank, smoking. Then we cycled to the cemetery.

We left our bicycles at the gate. We crossed a lawn, neatly mowed, and dotted with vases of flowers. I laid the flowers on the grass in front of my parents' headstone, and knelt down.

I read the words I knew by heart.

Arthur John O'Dell • Katherine Anne O'Dell
March 6, 1866 to February 20, 1902 • July 17, 1872 to February 20, 1902
A loving father and mother

"They died on the same day," said Henry.

"Their carriage was hit by a runaway horse in Toronto. They were on their way to the theatre."

"That's terrible."

I stood up. "I'm ready."

"Are you in a hurry?"

"Not really."

"Then I think I'd like to show you my mother's grave."

He was quiet as we walked to the newer part of the cemetery. He stopped by a patch of raw earth with a tall granite headstone. "This is it."

The black letters etched into the granite were sharp and clear.

Fanny Michelle Carter

August 6, 1867 to January 1,1908

Forever in our hearts

"I hate that we had to become Carters," said Henry. "As soon as I'm twenty-one, I'm changing my name back to McDougall, my father's name."

"What happened to your mother?" I said.

I added quickly, "You don't have to tell me."

"I'd like to but I just don't know where to start."

"What was she like? Start there."

"She was beautiful. The last time I saw her, she was getting dressed to go to a New Year's Eve party with Carter. I went upstairs to her bedroom to say good-bye. If I'd known what was going to happen, I'd have stayed with her. I don't even remember what we said to each other. I met some friends downtown and we went to a bar and then we watched the fireworks. I didn't even think about my mother."

He crouched down and stared at Fanny's headstone. "This is hard. I've actually never talked to anyone about this. It was getting light when I got back to the Gorge. I wasn't drunk. I never get drunk. An ambulance was there. And the police."

His face went pale. "Stella was waiting for me on the stairs. She had a letter. A boy brought it while I was out. It was for my mother, but Stella got it first. She read it to me. It was from Uncle Jacob. He said he was in love with my mother and that he was coming to the Gorge on New Year's Day to take us away. He was going to demand that Carter give her a divorce."

70

His voice broke. "Carter read the letter. He shot my mother and then he shot himself."

∼≈c

We walked in silence through the cemetery.

"Have you *ever* talked to Mr. Doyle about it?" I said finally.

"No."

"Have you even seen him?"

"At the funeral. But I walked away."

"If you would only let him –"

"Forget it, Charlotte." He grabbed my arm. "*Christ*, that's Stella. Stop. Don't move."

A bent-over figure, wearing black widow's weeds, a black bonnet and a veil of crepe, was walking along a gravel path, leaning on a cane. She stopped at a stone cross.

"That's Carter's grave," said Henry. "I see her here all the time but she never sees me."

Stella started to wail. It was eerie, not human. The back of my neck prickled.

"She made my mother's life hell." Henry stared at her. "She wanted to keep Carter for herself. Nothing my mother did was good enough. Stella hated that she was an actress. God, I despised living in that house. I used to beg to go to Uncle Jacob's on holidays and sometimes my mother let me. I know it hurt her."

The wailing stopped. Stella crossed the grass to the next grave. She raised her cane and struck a vase of red roses. The vase smashed into pieces and petals flew everywhere.

I gasped.

"Let's get out of here," said Henry.

Chapter Nineteen

The next morning, the Empire Day parade started at the head of Pandora Street. Henry and I pushed our bicycles through the crowds to get to a space near the front. Someone jostled me, shoving me up against Henry. He took my hand and held on as the drumbeats of the Fifth Regiment Band approached.

I was swept up in the excitement. Horses with gleaming coats and flowing manes and tails snorted and pranced. The mayor, in a silk hat and frock coat, stood in an open carriage. A little black dog with one brown ear followed, pulling a cart with a Union Jack. A troop of children, the girls in white pinafores and the boys in striped overalls, waved their flags.

Motor cars, led by a bright red car decorated with boughs of golden broom, passed us, honking their horns. Henry whooped and hollered. "That's *Scarlet Runner*. John Turner's driving it. His son's a friend of mine at *Saint Bartholomew's*. Hold onto my bicycle."

He ran beside the red car, shouting, and the driver, a plaid cap pulled low over his brow, laughed and waved.

We followed the parade as far as Government Street. Then we left it all behind and rode out to the inlet to watch the canoe races at the Regatta. I slid sideways peeks at Henry's strong tanned legs pumping the pedals until I nearly ran into the ditch and was only saved when he grabbed my handlebars!

We ended the day, tired and sunburnt, at Beacon Hill Park. The park was lit up with Chinese lanterns, stretching from tree to tree along the winding paths. Golden lights were reflected in the miniature lake. I had never seen anything so beautiful.

Rockets burst over our heads and filled the night sky with dazzling reds and silvers and purples. The St. Alice seemed a lifetime away.

I tipped my face upwards. The band struck up the notes of *God Save the King* as the outline of King Edward's head in lights blazed above us.

Henry swung me around, laughing.

And then he kissed me.

THE ST. ALICE HOTEL

1908

Chapter Twenty

As I changed out of my travelling clothes, Lizzie hung on every word.

"Is he awfully good looking?" she said.

"Yes."

"Did he kiss you?"

"Yes."

"Do you really like him?"

"I don't know," I said. "It's a bit confusing. I need to talk to Abigail."

"Can't. She's gone. She and her sister left suddenly on Saturday. Their father said Abigail could come back to England."

"I didn't even get to say good-bye!"

"She promised she'd write us a letter. Now, about Henry. If he's graduating, he's at least eighteen. Lucky you."

"Lizzie! I'll probably never see him again. He's in Victoria and I'm up here."

"Do you *want* to see him? That's what's important."

"I don't know. Some of the time, he was great fun. And then sometimes, he's so angry. I haven't told you the bad part yet."

"Let's go down to the beach."

"Now?"

"Why not? It's such a warm night and we can talk without Beatrice barging in."

We sat on a log. Far out on the water, a red light blinked. Four men were unloading a boat at the end of the dock, working by lanterns. On the boardwalk, a couple strolled by, murmuring.

I picked up a handful of pebbles and let them trickle through my fingers. I was all mixed up with the story of Henry and Fanny and Mr. Doyle. *Mr. Doyle*, who felt like a friend. I told Lizzie everything.

"What *exactly* did the letter say?" she said. "Tell me again."

"That Mr. Doyle loved Fanny and that he was coming to get Fanny and Henry on New Year's Day. He wanted her to get a divorce."

"And then Carter saw it and he shot Fanny and then himself. God, that's awful, Charlotte."

"I feel so sorry for Henry. But I'm sorry for Mr. Doyle too. He lost Fanny and now he's lost Henry. I can't choose sides!"

"Let's stay out for a while and walk." Lizzie sighed. "*Our* Mr. Doyle? I just can't believe it."

∽∾

I poured Mr. Doyle's tea. He looked so ordinary, folding his newspaper and setting it aside so I could put the tray down. The same Mr. Doyle, smiling at me. It was all so confusing.

"Charlotte, you found your aunt?"

"She's fine. It was just a trick to get me home for my birthday. She's...well..."

"A rascal?"

"Yes." I lifted the lid off his eggs. "Lizzie says you've been feeling poorly."

"She's exaggerating. I've lost some appetite, that's all. Now tell me, did you have a chance to post my letter?"

"I gave it right to Henry. I went to his school."

"You did? Did he write a reply?"

"No. I'm sorry."

Mr. Doyle picked up his knife and set it down again. "Did he seem well? How did he look?"

"Very well. He's quite tanned and he bicycles everywhere."

"Do you think he's eating properly?"

I laughed. "I have no idea, but I imagine he is."

"Did you like him?"

"Yes, of course."

"I *am* pleased."

"I've brought you something." I reached into the pocket of my apron and took out the blue bottle. "It's for malaria. I thought it might help."

"My dear girl, wherever did you get it?"

"From Sing Lee in Chinatown."

Mr. Doyle took the bottle from me and examined it.

"Sing Lee knows everything about traditional Chinese medicine."

"I'm sure he does."

"You must eat your eggs." I had put two on his breakfast tray.

"Must I?"

"You must."

Chapter Twenty-one

Later that morning, I went to the Bath House with messages for George from Mrs. Bannerman.

Mr. Doyle, in a white bath robe, was standing in front of the counter.

"I'm so pleased to see you this morning, Mr. Doyle." A broad smile crossed George's black face. "I've been asking where you've been. Knees acting up again?"

"My silly arthritis is a bit troublesome."

I wondered if he would mention the malaria, but he didn't.

"We'll soon fix you up."

George poured Mr. Doyle a glass of mineral water. "And now, Charlotte, what can I do for you?"

I recited my message, hoping I wasn't mixing it up. "Mr. Paisley's coming at two instead of three. Mrs. Peel's very sorry but she's had to cancel. She'll come tomorrow at ten. And Mrs. Howard would like a massage at five."

A door at the side of the room burst open. A cloud of steam gushed out, along with Colonel Mitterand. He had a white towel wrapped around his waist, and his chest, covered in black hair, gleamed with sweat.

"For God's sake, Mitterand," said Mr. Doyle. "There's a young girl here."

Colonel Mitterand glared at Mr. Doyle. He turned to George. "Boy, we've run out of towels."

"Sir, I'm just checking Mr. Doyle in. I'll be right –"

"I've never seen such a badly run establishment! I suppose they don't have bath houses in Africa."

Colonel Mitterand disappeared back into the steam.

"He's an ignorant man," said Mr. Doyle. "I'm sorry you heard that, Charlotte."

George laughed. "No matter. I was born and raised in Chicago. My mother's a school teacher."

⌒∿⌒

After lunch, Mrs. Wiggs sent me to the bar with a tray of clean glasses. Colonel Mitterand was slumped over the long counter, cradling a tumbler of whisky in his hands.

The bartender, Jack, a plump man with a round red face, was polishing the counter with a cloth. "Thank you Charlotte, love."

I started lining the glasses up in a neat row on a shelf.

"I could tell you things," slurred Colonel Mitterand. His words were garbled but one word stood out. "Doyle."

"Drink up, man," said Jack. "I'm closing for the afternoon."

"Doyle," repeated Colonel Mitterand. "We were in the same regiment. Oh yes, I could tell you things. High and mighty Doyle, looking down on me."

My hand froze on a glass. Was he talking about the Boer War in South Africa?

Colonel Mitterand spilled whisky down his waistcoat.

"Superior Mr. Doyle. If the guests in this hotel knew the truth, they'd have nothing to do with him. One word from me and he's finished."

"You're talking rubbish," said Jack. "Come on. Time to go."

The veins stood out on Colonel's Mitterand's nose. "The war was

78

no excuse. We all knew what he was doing. She was black. And she gave him a black son."

"Enough!" roared Jack.

"Thought no one would find out, didn't he? But I saw him. Five months ago on New Year's Day in London. Walking down the street with his arm around a black boy. They walked right past me. I heard the boy call him Papa."

"You were hung-over, man," said Jack.

"Not too hung-over to know what I saw. It's Doyle's dirty little secret. And he knows I know. He saw me too."

"Leave the glasses, Charlotte. Pay no attention to him."

I fled the bar.

~~~

I pulled Lizzie into the empty scullery and told her what Colonel Mitterand had said. "He makes me furious! What's wrong with Mr. Doyle having a black son?"

"Nothing. I think people should be able to fall in love with who-ever they want."

"Me too. But do you see what it means? That letter Henry's mother got on New Year's Eve? Mr. Doyle couldn't have sent it."

"Are you sure?"

"Whoever sent the letter said he was coming to get Fanny and Henry on New Year's Day. But Mr. Doyle was in London on New Year's Day. Colonel Mitterand saw him."

"Could he have made a mistake?"

"No. They both saw each other."

"So you think someone else wrote the letter and pretended to be Mr. Doyle?"

"No," I said slowly. "The letter must have been signed *Jacob*, not *Jacob Doyle*. I think there's another Jacob."

"That means that Henry's been blaming the wrong person."

"Yes! And Stella has too. She's horrid, Lizzie. Henry calls her a witch. We saw her in the cemetery. She was making this terrible crying sound and then she smashed a vase with her cane."

Lizzie shuddered. "What are you going to do?"

"Send Henry a telegram."

"I'll help pay for it. I've saved some of my wages from last week. What will you say?"

I thought hard.

"Mr. Doyle innocent. You must come."

Chapter Twenty-two

Boiling water overflowed the teapot.

"Land sake's child," said Mrs. Wiggs. "Pay attention. You're somewhere else far away."

"And she's letting Mr. Paisley's toast get cold," said Glenys. "It's been sitting there for ages."

"No need for you to get uppity, Glenys. Make him a fresh batch. And Charlotte, pull yourself together."

Annie shot me a sympathetic look as she squeezed past with a tray loaded with scrambled eggs.

"No tray for Mr. Doyle," said Mrs. Wiggs. "He's sent word that he doesn't want to be disturbed." She frowned. "He's missed far too many meals. I do wish Dr. Herman was here." The malaria medicine wasn't working. I picked up Mr. Paisley's plate of toast.

I'd persuaded Frank to send the telegram on his late run to Agassiz yesterday afternoon. Would Henry believe me? Please let him come. If Mr. Doyle could just see him, I knew he'd get better.

***

"Henry's here!" said Lizzie.

I was battling with my hair in front of the mirror.

"He's checking in this very minute. He just got off the omnibus. I heard him say his name to Miss Sweet. There can only be one Henry Carter, right?

I jumped up and raced down the stairs.

Henry was standing in front of the reception desk with his back to me. I didn't remember him being so tall. His shoulders were broad in his expensive looking overcoat and he wore a hat just like a gentleman.

"I'm here to see Mr. Doyle," he said.

"I'll put you in *San Francisco*," said Miss Sweet. "It's on the same floor, the second, right next door to Mr. Doyle."

"Is there another room? On a different floor?"

"Let me have a look...*London* on the first floor."

"That's better."

"You just missed Mr. Doyle. He went up to the Bath House. We're all relieved to see him up and about. He's feeling a little better."

Miss Sweet signaled to Clarence who was standing close by. "Clarence, take Mr. Carter's bag up to *London*. Now, shall I put you down for a table at dinner? Will you be dining with Mr. Doyle?"

"No...maybe...I don't know."

He turned and saw me. "Charlotte!"

"Hello, Henry."

"We need to talk. But not here. Let's go for a walk. Anywhere, just out of this hotel."

We walked through the front door, as if I were a guest. I prayed that Lizzie and Annie would cover for me.

As soon as we were on the boardwalk, Henry said, "What the bloody hell did you mean by that telegram?"

I blurted out the story.

"What are you saying? Uncle Jacob met a black woman in South Africa? And he has a son?"

"Yes."

"A *negro*? And where is this supposed son?"

"In London. At a boarding school."

"God, Charlotte. Why are you telling me all this?'

"Mr. Doyle couldn't have sent your mother that letter. He wasn't even in Victoria. He was in London. Colonel Mitterand saw him on New Year's Day. He was walking down the street with his son."

"A black boy."

"Yes."

"Some drunk in a bar is telling lies about Uncle Jacob and –"

"You didn't hear him. You weren't there."

"It can't be true. The letter was signed by Uncle Jacob."

"I'll bet you it was signed by another Jacob but not Jacob Doyle. You don't use last names in a love letter. There must be another Jacob. There has to be."

"My mother and I were so close. I would have known."

"You're her son. She wouldn't have wanted you to know."

Henry put his head between his hands.

"Mr. Doyle is ill. He needs to see you."

"If he's so sick, then why doesn't he go to a doctor?"

"Doctor Herman is away in Vancouver. He won't be back until tomorrow. Please, Henry. Talk to Mr. Doyle."

Chapter Twenty-three

"His name was Jacob Painter," said Henry.

After dining alone with Mr. Doyle in his room, he met me on the beach. I had changed out of my uniform, and pinned the robin brooch on my blouse.

"My mother was having an affair with Painter. Uncle Jacob knew him. He was an actor in the play my mother was in. He warned my mother to be careful. But he never believed that Carter would kill her. Never."

I clasped Henry's arm. He slid his hand up and took mine.

"Now I know what really happened," he said. "I think I saw Painter at my mother's funeral. There was a man standing at the back. He was crying. I'd never seen him before."

"Oh, Henry. If only he hadn't sent that letter!"

"But he did. Uncle Jacob says Painter was a bloody fool. He was so besotted with my mother he didn't think about what might happen if Carter saw it. Uncle Jacob didn't even know about the letter until I told him. He was shocked. He couldn't understand why I wouldn't see him."

"Is he angry?"

"No. He's overjoyed that we're friends again."

"Is he mad at me for telling you?"

"Not at all."

"Did he talk about his son?"

Henry flushed. "Some. His name is Musa. He's seven. His mother still lives in South Africa but Uncle Jacob has sent him to a boarding school in London. I don't understand why he did that. And about this woman –"

"Maybe he loved her," I said.

"Charlotte. She's black."

I was silent.

"I'll stay here at the St. Alice for a while," said Henry. "There's nothing going on at school anyway. Exams are over. I want Uncle Jacob to see this Doctor Herman as soon as he's back. It's probably the malaria again but still, he looks terrible...What's the matter? You're not even listening."

"It's the way you talk about black people."

"*What?*"

"As if they're inferior."

"That's not true." He sighed. "Look, I don't *dislike* black people. I just think white people and black people shouldn't mix together. That's normal, isn't it?"

"Do you feel the same way about Chinese people?"

"Yes, I do."

"But you were quite happy to eat chocolate cake with Mr. Chang."

"*That* was different."

"Why?"

Henry picked up a rock and threw it. "Because...I don't know. He's your aunt's boarder."

"Do you even *know* any black people?"

"No."

"Then you should go to the Bath House and talk to George. He's black."

"And why would I want to do that?"

I didn't say anything.

"Dammit, Charlotte. Now you're making me think about things."

Before we went inside, I picked a handful of peppermint leaves from the garden. "I'll make Mr. Doyle some tea. He likes it. He says it settles his stomach."

We went into the kitchen through the back door.

"What a lark!" said Henry. "I'm going to skulk around like a servant."

"Servants don't skulk, Henry."

The kitchen was deserted with only one dim light on. While I steeped the leaves in a teapot, Henry poked around in the cupboards and drawers. He spotted one of Mr. Pincer's tall white chef's hats and stuck it on his head.

I couldn't help laughing. "Stop! Someone might come in."

Henry crackled with energy. "I want to celebrate that Uncle Jacob are I are friends again. What's there to do around here that's fun?"

"Some of the staff are having a bonfire on the beach tonight. The boys have gathered a huge pile of driftwood. It's the first party of the summer."

"A staff party? Sounds a little dubious. Will there be beer?"

"Clarence and Fred are bringing some."

Henry peered over my shoulder. "Is Uncle Jacob really going to drink that?"

"Of course." I put the teapot and a cup and saucer on a tray. "I'm going to take this up and then I've still got some chores to finish. I'll meet you on the boardwalk at ten o'clock. And don't be late."

Henry saluted.

"Tea," said Mr. Doyle. "You read my mind. I was just about – Charlotte. Your brooch. Where did you get it?"

"Aunt Ginny gave it to me for my birthday. It was such a surprise.

It belonged to my mother. I never thought it would be mine."

"Your mother. Katherine. I'm sorry. I'm staring. It's just that it's so unusual."

"I know. I can't stop looking at it either. Do you think the rubies are real?"

"Yes, I do. And the beak and the eye are onyx. It's very beautiful. Do you remember your mother wearing it?"

"Sometimes." Should I tell him it had been a secret, hidden in my mother's night table? That she had only worn it when my father was away?

"Well, it's a lovely treasure."

"I'm afraid I might lose it. Lizzie loves it too. She said I should sew it on with thread. I'd wear it all the time if I could but I'm not allowed to wear it on my uniform."

"The mighty Mrs. Bannerman. She keeps you girls in line," said Mr. Doyle. "You look like you're going out tonight."

"A beach party. We're going to have a bonfire. It's for the staff but Henry's coming too."

He smiled. "What fun."

Chapter Twenty-four

The boardwalk was lit by flickering torches. I waited for Henry by the beach stairs. Dance music spilled over from the pavilion. Far down the beach, the bonfire glowed.

"You've been ages," I said, when Henry finally wandered up. "We're missing everything."

"Sorry."

"Where have you been?"

He poked me in the ribs. "If you must know, at the Bath House talking to George."

"Really?"

"Yes."

"What did you talk about?"

"Baseball, mostly. He's from Chicago. He's a Cubs fan. He plays on a team in Agassiz. If I was staying here much longer, I'd play a few games with them."

We started walking down the beach. Stars sprinkled the sky and the moon hadn't come up yet. Pebbles rolled under our feet. Beside us the lake was smooth and black.

"I still can't believe it," said Henry. "Uncle Jacob wants me to apply to some American universities. Harvard and Yale. And we're going to Europe in August. Paris, Florence and Rome."

"Char!" called Lizzie. "At last!"

Figures stood around the bonfire, moving in and out of shadows. Someone had dragged up logs to sit on. Lizzie was standing beside

James, one of the grooms. She pulled me over. "I thought you weren't coming."

"This is Henry," I said. "Henry, this is Lizzie and James. And that's Mike and Rachel."

James nodded.

"Hey, Henry," said Mike.

"You might as well stop right there," said Henry. "I'll never remember all these names."

Nobody said anything. James held out a bottle of beer. "Want one?"

"Why not?" Henry took a beer and slid his arm around my waist.

Everyone was looking. I stiffened.

"Relax," he whispered.

I held my hands out to the flames. In seconds, my face burned but my back was cold. The conversation drifted from Model T cars to the Lumberjack Days in August. Lizzie wandered off and sat on a log beside Ardis. Henry drank his beer slowly and didn't say a word.

There was a scuffle in the dark down by the water. Shouting and a great splash.

Bridie yelled, "Get Clarence! Clarence next!"

A dripping James appeared out of the shadows, crept up behind Lizzie and shook himself like a wet dog.

Lizzie leaped up. "Get away! You're soaking me!"

Henry kissed my hair. "Why is that fellow staring at us?"

"Who?"

"Over there. The one drinking all the beer."

"That's Mop."

"Mop?" Henry snorted.

"Don't. He'll hear you."

Lizzie, Ardis and Rachel burst into laughter. I glanced over at them. They were having so much fun.

"Watch this." Fred picked up a thin stick and lit the end in the flames. He tilted the stick and the fire crawled up towards his fingers.

"Let go, idiot," said Rachel.

Fred dropped the stick.

"Baby." Mop grabbed a stick from the ground and lit it.

"This is so stupid," said Lizzie.

We were all watching the burning stick. The end glowed red and broke off. The bit near Mop's fingers flared.

"Ouch!" Mop waved his hand in the air. "Damn!"

Henry laughed.

Mop picked up his bottle of beer. "I thought this was a staff party. Since when do hotel guests come to staff parties?"

"Mop," said Mike. "You're drinking too much, man."

Mop spun around and disappeared down the beach. I strained to see where he was going. A few minutes later, he staggered back, his arms wrapped around an enormous stump. He walked right up to the fire, lifted the stump over his head and dropped it straight down.

Chunks of burning wood flew into the air. Sparks showered down.

"Jesus," said Henry. "Are you trying to set us on fire? Come on, Charlotte. Let's go."

We didn't talk as we walked back to the boardwalk. The party was ruined. I didn't even care that we had left.

Behind us, a voice demanded, "What are you doing with Charlotte?"

We turned around. It was Mop, clutching a bottle, his face lit up by a torch.

"You're drunk," said Henry.

Mop dropped the bottle and shoved Henry in the chest.

"Mop, stop!" I said.

Mop swung his fist at Henry. Henry grabbed his arm and twisted it. He punched Mop in the face.

Mop grunted. He sprawled on the boardwalk. He staggered to his feet, blood pouring from his nose. "Bastard."

He jumped off the boardwalk and vanished.

Henry kicked at the pieces of broken beer bottle. "God, what a night."

Chapter Twenty-five

I stared at my bowl of porridge, then shoved it away. Before I could leave, Lizzie, Rachel and Bridie plunked down at the table.

"So, Charlotte," said Bridie. "What happened to Mop last night?"

Lizzie busied herself stirring brown sugar into her porridge. We had stumbled into bed after midnight and I'd refused to discuss the party.

I shrugged.

"He had a bloody nose," said Rachel. "And his cheek is cut. He said Henry tried to beat him up." She paused. "Charlotte's boyfriend."

"He's not my boyfriend. And you heard Mop. He was so rude to Henry, telling him he shouldn't have come."

"Maybe he was right," said Bridie.

I stared at her. She flushed. "I mean, we've never had hotel guests at our parties before. You're new here. Maybe you didn't know that."

"How long is Henry staying?" said Rachel.

"I have no idea. And in case you hadn't noticed, Mop was drunk. He started the fight. Henry was just defending himself."

"Mop is the nicest boy here," said Bridie. "What do you think, Lizzie?"

"I'm staying out of this."

"I've *never* seen Mop drink like that," said Rachel.

I stood up. "I know you all think Mop is perfect but actually, he's not."

I grabbed my bowl and left.

When I collected Mr. Doyle's breakfast tray, his eggs and toast were gone. He had even scraped the last bit of marmalade from the fancy jar. He had wiped up the crumbs and stacked his dishes and the empty jar on his tray.

"Mr. Doyle! You ate all your breakfast! Is the malaria going away?"

"I believe it is."

Mr. Timmins was at the door when I left.

"There you are, Philip," said Mr. Doyle. "Come in, come in. Charlotte, Mr. Timmins and I are having an important meeting this morning. We don't wish to be disturbed, except for some coffee at eleven o'clock."

It sounded so official. I'd often seen them with their heads together, deep in conversation. I wondered what they were talking about this time.

As I shut the door quietly behind me, I heard Mr. Doyle say, "We'll leave the room for Effie to clean and go to the library. I must get this new will settled this morning."

⁓

"Girls, we'll set the tea out in the downstairs parlour this afternoon," said Mrs. Wiggs. "Mr. Wiggs says there's going to be a big storm later today."

When the last cups and saucers were cleared from the parlour, I took my break. A whole hour to compose a letter to Abigail.

I left through the kitchen door, praying I wouldn't see Mop. The omnibus was parked behind the hotel. Mike was polishing the brass horn. Henry watched, his back to me, his hands in his pockets. He said something and Mike laughed.

I hurried around the side of the hotel and across the boardwalk to the beach stairs. A stiff wind blew, churning the lake into a sea of whitecaps. I sat on a log. My hair had fallen down and the wind whipped it around my face.

How should I start?

I tried it out loud. *Dear Abigail, All the girls hate me.*

It sounded so childish. I tried again.

Mop is jealous which is infuriating because he's not my boyfriend.

I stopped. It was impossible to find the right words.

Henry thinks —

I had no idea what Henry thought.

I wish I'd never met him.

Was that true?

I groaned. I was sick of the whole thing. I watched two sailboats race across the lake. The Howards, bundled up, waved to me from the end of the dock.

I was freezing. I stood up. Lizzie was the writer. I'd ask her to help me.

Lizzie had abandoned me. I'd wanted her so much to stand up for me when the girls were criticizing Henry, but she hadn't.

My eyes stung.

∽∾c

Her eyes red and puffy, Mrs. Wiggs was buttoning her coat. "Come on, Ina and Flora. It's time to go. Mr. Pincer will be here soon. I don't see how I can leave you girls right now but Mr. Wiggs needs his dinner."

"I can't remember anything I'm supposed to do," said Annie. "I can't think straight."

"Please don't leave us with Mr. Pincer," said Lizzie.

Mrs. Wiggs unbuttoned her coat. "Ina and Flora, you go out to the wagon and tell Mr. Wiggs I'll be here for a while and he should take you home. And there's no need for you two to cry."

She put her apron back on. "Lizzie, take some tea up to Effie. Make it strong with lots of sugar. Keep her company and make sure she doesn't do anything silly."

"What's wrong with Effie?" I said. "What's happened?"

"It's Mr. Doyle," said Glenys. "Effie found him. He's dead."

Chapter Twenty-six

I ran after Lizzie into the hall. "What happened?"

"Effie's in a terrible state. Says she's never seen a dead person before. She thought Mr. Doyle was napping and she started straightening up and then wondered if she should come back later. She was supposed to turn down his bed but he was already in his bed and she didn't know what to do. You know Effie. She's terrified of making Mrs. Bannerman cross. Then she saw a puddle of vomit on the floor and looked at his face. His eyes were open but he wasn't looking at anything and she said she just knew he was dead."

"Oh God, Lizzie."

Lizzie shifted the tea tray in her arms. "Effie's got me so rattled I can't think straight. They've locked Mr. Doyle's room and no one can go in. I heard Mr. Brown tell Mrs. Bannerman that Doctor Herman's coming back on the train today from Vancouver and Mr. Brown has gone to meet him. But it's not going to do any good, is it? It's too late."

"Do you know where Henry is?"

"I saw him coming out of Mr. Brown's office. But I don't know where he went."

My head reeled.

"Effie keeps going on about something not being her fault. She won't stop crying. I'd better take this tea up. Mr. Brown said that no matter what, the hotel must keep running. He doesn't want the guests upset."

"The guests! Doesn't he care about Mr. Doyle?"

"He says that we're not supposed to talk about it among ourselves but he's never going to stop us. He wants to keep it a secret but I don't see how. Everyone's going to be talking about it. Especially the guests."

~~

I crossed the lobby, passing Mr. Brown and a thin man with a short brown beard. Dr. Herman, I thought.

The hotel felt empty, except for a low murmur of voices in the downstairs parlour. I escaped through the front door, not caring if Mrs. Bannerman saw me. The verandah was deserted. I took a blanket from the blanket box and wrapped it around my shoulders.

A flowerpot tipped over in the wind. The rain started, spattering on the dusty ground.

Mr. Doyle. My eyes spilled over with tears. How did this happen? He said his malaria was getting better. He'd eaten all his breakfast. I couldn't understand it. And I just couldn't believe he was dead.

I saw Henry trudging up the road, leaning into the rain and wind. I ran to meet him. "Where have you been?"

"Walking." Henry had no hat and his wet hair was plastered to his head. "I've been on the road to Agassiz. I didn't know where else to go. I didn't see anyone, not even a cart and horse. I've walked for miles and miles."

"You must be frozen."

"Do you know about Uncle Jacob?"

"Yes," I whispered.

"What am I going to do?"

"Doctor Herman's here. Talk to him."

Chapter Twenty-seven

I served the morning coffee on the verandah. The storm had passed and the lake sparkled under a bright blue sky. The guests talked in low voices. Everyone knew about Mr. Doyle.

Henry sat by himself, at the far end of the verandah. I brought his coffee. His face was grey, with dark smudges under his eyes. "Sit for a minute."

"I'll get in trouble –"

"Forget the damn rules. No one's even looking over here."

I lowered myself onto a chair, ready to leap up at any second.

"I talked to Dr. Herman," said Henry. "He's not satisfied it was malaria. He's ordered an autopsy. They're taking Uncle Jacob to Chilliwack and someone called Dr. Markham will do it." His voice shook. "They're going to cut Uncle Jacob open and see what killed him."

I nearly fainted at the sound of it. "If it wasn't malaria, what was it?"

"I don't know. Dr. Herman said there was a blue bottle of liquid in his room. He couldn't identify it. He said it didn't look like anything a real doctor would prescribe."

My palms were sweaty. "Henry, I –"

A horse whinnied. A covered carriage rattled to a stop in front of the St. Alice. A driver sat in front, holding the reins. On the side of the carriage was a big red cross and the word Ambulance.

"What's happening?" quavered Mr. Paisley. "Can someone tell me what's happening?"

Two attendants hopped out of the back of the ambulance carrying a stretcher.

"Dear God," said Mrs. Bice, pressing a lace trimmed handkerchief to her eye.

Mrs. Hawthorne gave a sob.

"Has anyone talked to Mr. Timmins?" said Mrs. Peel. "He'll know more about it."

Colonel Mitterand slurped his coffee. "Poor chap. Rotten luck, malaria."

Mr. Brown rushed out the front door of the hotel, waving his arms. "Not here! Take it to the back!"

"That blue bottle?" said Henry. "They need to find out what was in it."

He pushed away his coffee.

"It killed Uncle Jacob."

✑

Henry sat with Mr. Timmins at lunch. Both of them barely sipped their soup. They were the last to leave the dining room.

On the way out, Henry said to me, "Mr. Timmins and I are going out in his motor car for the rest of the day. Anything to get away from this damn hotel."

I didn't even say good-bye. The blue bottle. It was all I could think about. Was the malaria medicine poisonous? Had Sing Lee made a mistake? Had Mr. Doyle even taken it?

Did I kill Mr. Doyle? A tray of wine glasses slipped out of my hands and crashed on the floor. Broken glass sprayed everywhere.

I burst into tears.

Annie pushed open the swinging door, took one look and said. "I'll get a broom."

Chapter Twenty-eight

I woke up Monday morning, my head throbbing. I stayed in bed until the last minute. Lizzie got me a damp cool facecloth and laid it across my forehead.

Mrs. Wiggs watched me stumble about the kitchen. "Take this fresh pot of tea to the Peels in the library, then I want you to have a lie-down. We can manage until after lunch without you."

I passed through the lobby with the tea. A trunk was waiting by the front door, four brown leather suitcases stacked next to it. Beatrice sat on the trunk, a white and green striped hat box on her lap, her eyes flashing back and forth.

"We're leaving today," she announced.

I'd finally have Lizzie to myself again. But I was going to miss Mrs. Chisholm.

"I was up all night, looking after Mrs. Chisholm. Another migraine. I didn't sleep a wink."

"Right."

"How can respectable people stay in a hotel where guests die? Who's going to be next? I can tell you one thing, it won't be me."

Mrs. Chisholm appeared at the bottom of the staircase, her face hidden by a heavy veil.

Beatrice jumped up and flounced past me. "I won't miss one thing about this hotel!"

Mr. Timmins wanted coffee in the upstairs parlour. He was reading the *British Colonist* when I set down his tray.

A bold headline jumped out at me.

DEATH AT THE ST. ALICE HOTEL

"How are you holding up?" he said.

"I don't know. I just wish I knew what was going to happen."

"I sent a telegram to Mr. Doyle's sister in San Francisco. Her name is Mrs. Carpenter. She'll be here on Friday. I'll be reading the will, Charlotte. I want you to be there.'"

"Me, sir?"

"Yes."

Had Mr. Doyle left me something? His chess set?

"In the meantime," said Mr. Timmins, "Dr. Markham has informed me there is going to be an inquest. There'll be a coroner and a jury. Dr. Markham will present his findings from the autopsy. And other people will speak as well."

"Does Henry know?"

"Yes, I've told him. He'll want to be there."

"Will you be speaking?'"

"Yes, I'm sure I will."

"And Dr. Herman?"

"Most definitely."

He'll talk about the blue bottle. My stomach clenched. "Does having an inquest mean they think something is wrong?"

Mr. Timmins frowned slightly. "It means it's not as straightforward as we hoped."

He patted my shoulder. "But there is no need for you to worry."

◦◦◦

Mrs. Bannerman called me to her office after dinner.

"The Coroner has contacted Mr. Brown. He's given him a list of who is to go to the inquest tomorrow. He wants to include the staff members who specifically looked after Mr. Doyle. That's you and Effie."

"Just us?"

"I told Mr. Brown it's ridiculous but there's nothing I can do about it."

"Will we have to say anything?"

"I don't know. But we'll be short of staff again. I find it vexing, Charlotte, how time after time you manage to evade your duties. Chess games with Mr. Doyle, a trip to Victoria, Mrs. Wiggs excused you from waitressing this morning, and now this."

"That's not fair."

"At this inquest, I'll expect you and Effie to remember your place. You are representing the St. Alice. There'll be no need to volunteer your opinions. A simple yes or no will do."

"Will you be there?"

"Of course."

My thoughts in a turmoil, I left the office. When I got to our room, Effie was on my bed, crying.

"She won't stop," said Lizzie. "She's going on and on about having to go to the inquest."

"It's all right, Effie," I said. "I'll be there too."

"I didn't touch anything in his room," said Effie.

What on earth was she talking about? I wanted to be alone with Lizzie to talk to her about the blue bottle.

"You have to go now," I said.

Sniffing, Effie stumbled to the door. "I just know I'll faint."

Chapter Twenty-nine

The inquest was held in the post office in Agassiz. Frank drove me, Effie, Mr. Brown and Mrs. Bannerman in the omnibus. Mr. Timmins and Henry followed in Mr. Timmins's motor car.

A young man in a tan uniform with a Sheriff badge checked our names off a list as we filed through the post office door. A man in a dark suit with a stiff white collar sat behind a table at the front of the room. The Coroner, I thought. There was a black Bible, a gavel and a jug of water and glasses on the table. A Union Jack and a portrait of King Edward hung on the wall.

Eight men sat on chairs at the side. I recognized Mr. Inkman, who owned *Inkman's* store, the preacher who sometimes came to the St. Alice on Sundays and Mr. Wiggs. The rest of the men looked like farmers in their boots and overalls.

Straight-backed chairs were lined up in two rows. They were already half filled with women in plain hats, some with shopping baskets.

"They shouldn't let the public in," muttered Mrs. Bannerman. "This isn't a spectacle. I want you girls to sit with me. And no histrionics, Effie."

Effie and I sat on either side of Mrs. Bannerman. Mr. Timmins and Henry were in front of us, next to Doctor Herman who was talking to a tall white haired man seated beside him. Doctor Markham? Mr. Brown stayed standing at the back next to a policeman in uniform and a man scribbling in a notebook.

The Coroner cleared his throat. "We are here today to determine the circumstances of Mr. Jacob Doyle's death at the St Alice Hotel on Saturday, May 30. I expect order in the proceedings at all times." He consulted a paper. "I call the first witness, Doctor Markham."

The white haired man stood up and walked to the front of the room. The Sheriff held the Bible and directed Doctor Markham to place his hand on it. "Do you swear to tell the truth, the whole truth and nothing but the truth, so help you God?"

"I do."

"Please take your seat."

Doctor Markham sat on a chair beside the Coroner's table.

"State your full name and occupation," said the Coroner.

"Abraham Markham, physician. I conducted the autopsy on Jacob Doyle on June 1."

The Coroner leaned forward. "What did you find?"

"The deceased was a middle-aged male in overall good health. His brain, liver, lungs and kidneys were normal. I found substantial fatty tissue around the heart indicating the presence of heart disease."

"In your opinion, is that what killed him?"

"No. The heart disease had not progressed sufficiently to cause death."

"Go on."

Everyone in the room was still. A fly banged against a window and the overhead fan creaked.

"He died from an overdose of digitalis."

The room buzzed. Digitalis? I had never heard of it.

"There is no possibility he died from malaria?"

"None. It was definitely digitalis," said Doctor Markham. "Digitalis is an extract from the foxglove plant. It is used to treat heart disease. A correct dose would be a safe treatment for Mr. Doyle's heart condition. But I found excessive amounts, enough to kill him."

I was confused. Aunt Ginny knew a child who had died chewing some foxglove leaves. How could something made from a poisonous plant like foxgloves be a medicine?

"I call Dr. Joseph Herman," said the Coroner.

"Jacob Doyle and I were friends for many years," said Dr. Herman. "But I was not his doctor."

"Were you aware if he was taking digitalis?"

"No. "

"Did you find any medicines in his room?"

"I found Mr. Doyle's arthritis tablets on his night table and a blue bottle, containing an unknown liquid, in the back of a cupboard."

"An unknown liquid? How is digitalis dispensed?"

"It is dispensed as a liquid. The label on the bottle must clearly set out the dose and how often it must be taken."

"Does the blue bottle have a label?"

"Yes, but it is all in Chinese characters. I am not able to decipher it."

"We'll get the contents analyzed." The Coroner made a note. "What are the symptoms of digitalis poisoning?"

"Headache, nausea, weakness, loss of appetite, blurry vision," said Dr. Herman.

I flinched. Mr. Doyle had them all.

"I call Charlotte O'Dell."

My hand shook on the Bible.

"Are you the maid who brought Mr. Doyle his breakfast?"

"Yes."

"Did you take his breakfast the day he died?"

"Yes."

"Did he eat the breakfast?"

"Yes, he ate all of it. Toast, eggs and he'd even finished off his jar of marmalade."

"Did he appear ill?"

"No. Lots of days he did but not that morning. I was so pleased he was feeling better."

Mrs. Bannerman caught my eye and slightly shook her head.

It was over. I returned to my chair, my legs weak.

"I'll call Evelyn Robertson." Effie gasped. Mrs. Bannerman gave her a nudge.

"You found Mr. Doyle?" said the Coroner.

"Yes."

"Speak up. I can't hear you."

"*Yes.*"

"Why were you in his room in the afternoon? Were you cleaning?"

"No. I did that in the morning. I went back to turn down his bed." Effie sobbed. "He was always so nice to me. He picked up his own towels."

"What did you find?"

"He had thrown up on the floor. He was in his bed."

"Did you know he was dead?" said the Coroner.

"Yes."

"How?"

"I just did."

"You called for help?"

"I got Mrs. Bannerman."

"No further questions. I call Mr. Philip Timmins."

Mr. Timmins's limp was more pronounced as he walked to the front of the room. "My name is Philip Timmins and I am a lawyer."

"What was your relationship with Mr. Doyle?"

"We were friends. We talked about many things. Business, politics."

"Did you perform any professional duties?"

"He asked me to prepare a will."

"A will? When was this done?"

"The morning he died. He felt ill by the time we finished but he was determined to do it. And in my opinion, he was mentally capable of doing so."

"Why the urgency? Was he worried about dying?"

"Not that I was aware of."

"Was he depressed?"

Henry jumped up. "I know what you're implying! You think Uncle Jacob killed himself on purpose!"

"Sit down, young man."

"He was happy. We were planning to go to Europe."

"If you don't sit down, I will have you removed."

Henry sank back on his chair.

The Coroner turned back to Mr. Timmins.

"Was Mr. Doyle depressed?"

"Definitely not."

"Was he worried?"

"No. Quite the opposite. He was excited about something but I am not at liberty to speak about it."

"Was Mr. Doyle a careless man? Could he have made a mistake with his dosage?"

"No. Meticulous, I would say. I remind you that Doctor Herman found no digitalis in his room."

The coroner examined a paper. "Very well. We have enough evidence for the jury to reach a verdict as to cause of death."

The eight jurors got up and shuffled into a back room. There was nothing for the rest of us to do but wait.

Chapter Thirty

In less than half an hour, the jurors were back in their seats. They were so quick. My heart raced. What did that mean?

"Members of the jury, have you reached a verdict?" said the Coroner.

Mr. Wiggs stood up, mopping his forehead with a handkerchief. "Murder. That's what we've decided. Murder."

The room exploded with cries of disbelief.

"Everyone calm down!" The Coroner glared at the jury. "This is completely unacceptable. There has been no suggestion of murder. The only question before you today is whether an overdose of digitalis killed Jacob Doyle. That is all."

"Murder," repeated Mr. Wiggs. "We've made up our mind."

"No!" said Henry.

Mr. Timmins shook his head and Doctor Herman groaned.

"Not in my hotel!" shouted Mr. Brown.

"Quiet!" roared the Coroner. "This verdict cannot stand. Members of the jury, you were never asked to –"

"We know what we heard," said Mr. Wiggs.

"Death by digitalis overdose." The Coroner banged his gavel. "So ordered."

◆

"It was horrible, Lizzie."

We had brought cups of tea up to our room and were sitting on our beds in our nightgowns.

"How did Henry take it?"

"Terribly. You should have seen his face. I haven't even been able to talk to him. He's been with Mr. Timmins ever since we got back."

"Murder," said Lizzie. "At the St. Alice. I've got goosebumps."

Chapter Thirty-one

I slept in again the next morning.

Lizzie came to get me. "Don't worry. Mrs. Wiggs said it's understandable after the inquest and everything."

She sat on her bed while I put on my uniform and straightened my cap. "Everyone's leaving. Miss Sweet says the telephone keeps ringing with people cancelling their reservations. The Peels are going tomorrow."

"The Howards?"

"They're staying. Mrs. Howard is trying to organize a picnic to cheer everyone up but no one wants to go."

"Lizzie, about what happened...I mean, at the bonfire..."

"Forget it. I have. And you know that poor honeymoon couple staying in *Florence*? She can't stop crying."

⁓

The widows asked for coffee in the library. "And something sweet," said Gertie, who delivered their message to the kitchen.

I passed through the lobby with their tray. Colonel Mitterand was leaning over Miss Sweet's desk. "I must go *now*."

"But the omnibus has already left," said Miss Sweet.

"Send word to that driver to come back immediately!"

Miss Sweet's hands fluttered. "Oh my. I can't –"

Colonel Mitterand banged his fist on the desk. "I'm not staying in a hotel where guests are poisoned!"

Mr. Brown bustled out of his office. "What seems to be the problem?"

"Damn sloppy regiment you're running, Brown," steamed Colonel Mitterand.

Mr. Brown glanced around the lobby. "There's no need to...come to the bar and Jack will pour you a whisky."

Colonel Mitterand humphed and stomped away.

Mr. Brown stared at the front door. I turned to look. Two men walked in. One was quite old, with rumpled clothes and grey hair, and the other was young, dressed in a snappy black suit and smoking a cigarette.

They strode up to the reception desk.

"Detective Bentley," said the older man. "I've come over from Mission. This is Detective Quinn, my colleague from Vancouver."

"We're going to interview the staff," said Detective Quinn. "I suggest we start with your receptionist." He gave Miss Sweet an icy smile. "You must have your eye on everything that goes on in this hotel."

Miss Sweet gave a little yelp.

"You mustn't disturb my guests," said Mr. Brown.

"We'll make that decision, not you."

Mr. Brown glared at me. "Stop gaping, young lady, and get back to your duties."

⌇

Mrs. Bannerman, eyes blazing, came to the kitchen and called us one by one.

Ina and Flora were only gone a few minutes. They came back wide-eyed. "An old man asked us to say our names," said Flora, "and when Ina wouldn't talk, I answered for her and the old man smiled and said that was fine and that there was nothing to be nervous about."

"I didn't like the other man," whispered Ina. "He stared."

"Not too bad," said Lizzie when she returned. "Not scary or anything. Kind of rushed."

"Disappointing," said Annie. "I thought it would be more exciting. They just wanted to know if I had anything to tell them." She sighed. "Couldn't think of anything."

"Of course not," said Mrs. Wiggs. "You're good girls, all of you. Mr. Wiggs says that he'll have something to say if the police start blaming my kitchen."

Mrs. Bannerman came to the door.

"Charlotte," she said.

Chapter Thirty-two

I stood outside Mr. Brown's office door, smoothing my hands across my apron. I knocked and a voice said, "Come in."

The older detective was seated at Mr. Brown's desk. "Charlotte O'Dell?"

"Yes sir."

"Please sit down."

I sat on the edge of a hard wood chair. "I'm Detective Bentley and this is Detective Quinn." He nodded at the dark haired man who was leaning against the wall, staring out the window. An unlit cigarette dangled between his fingers. "We have a few questions to ask you."

I barely heard him. I was trying desperately not to look at the blue bottle sitting in the middle of Mr. Brown's desk.

"What is your position here at the St. Alice, Charlotte?"

"I'm a waitress, sir."

I remembered what Mrs. Bannerman said before the inquest. *There's no need to volunteer your opinion. A simple yes or no will do.* This time, I vowed to follow her advice.

"How long have you worked here?"

"I started at the end of April."

"Are you happy here?"

"Yes."

"Any problems with the cook, Mrs..." He checked the paper. "Mrs. Wiggs?"

"No, sir."

"The housekeeper Mrs. Bannerman treat you fairly?"

"Yes."

"How do you get along with the guests?"

"Fine."

Detective Bentley smiled. "You're doing well, Charlotte."

"So you get along with the guests fine." Detective Quinn walked across the room until he was standing right beside me. "Fine enough to play chess with Mr. Doyle. Tell us about it."

"There's nothing to tell," I stammered. "He asked me, that's all. We only played once."

"A waitress playing chess with a guest? Did Mrs. Bannerman approve?"

"It made her angry. But Mr. Doyle insisted."

"Did you wonder why he wanted to spend time with you?"

"I did at first. But then I thought it was just because he liked a good game of chess. He found out I played chess well, that was all."

I bit my lip. I was talking too much.

"He found out when you brought him his breakfast trays."

"I...yes."

"He only wanted *you* to bring his breakfast. *I want Charlotte O'Dell*, he said. None of the other girls would do."

"No...I mean, I don't know. Mrs. Wiggs just said for me to do it."

"As if you and he knew each other from before."

"No! I never met Mr. Doyle until I came here."

"But you liked him, didn't you?"

I didn't say anything. I wanted Detective Bentley to ask the questions.

"And you and Mr. Doyle used to chat. About things like chess."

"Yes."

He was talking so fast that I wasn't ready for his next question. He picked up the blue bottle. "Have you seen this before?"

I looked at Detective Bentley.

"Have you seen it before?" repeated Detective Quinn.

My throat was so dry I couldn't speak.

"That's not a difficult question. The other girls were able to answer."

"Yes...yes." I swallowed. "I...I gave it to Mr. Doyle."

I closed my eyes. Why did I say that?

Detective Quinn leaned his face close to mine. "Tell us."

I stared at my hands. "I bought it in Chinatown. From Sing Lee. It's malaria medicine. That's what he told me."

Detective Quinn raised his eyebrows. "And you believed a Chinaman?"

I glared at him. "I believed Sing Lee."

"We've sent the contents away for analyzing," said Detective Bentley. "But we need to know exactly when and where you purchased it."

I turned to him eagerly. He would understand. "On the Empire Day weekend. I was in Victoria. I went to Sing Lee's shop to get some herbs for my aunt. I asked Sing Lee if he had medicine for malaria. Mr. Doyle said he had malaria. I wanted to help."

"You started working here at the St. Alice a month ago and you have already made a trip back to Victoria," said Detective Quinn. "Homesick so soon?"

"My aunt was missing. I got a telegram."

"So, you went to Victoria to find a missing aunt. Are you sure it wasn't to visit Sing Lee's shop?"

"No. I didn't even know I would be going there."

"But you knew the shop well. You'd been there before. You knew what kinds of things Sing Lee sold. Isn't that right, Charlotte?"

"Yes."

"That's enough," said Detective Bentley.

I stood up. "The blue bottle, sir. The contents. When will you know what it is?"

"We'll know in two days."

Chapter Thirty-three

Pots banged. Bacon spat. The kitchen smelled like currant buns. No matter what happened, Mrs. Wiggs made breakfast.

She wiped her floury hands on her apron. "Charlotte, nip outside and get some parsley for the Eggs Benedict."

The parsley grew in the kitchen garden behind the strawberry beds. I picked up a basket and some scissors.

The two detectives were standing in front of the greenhouse, talking to Mr. Bains.

I stopped beside the peas.

Detective Bentley looked up and saw me. My cheeks burned as I walked along the path to the parsley patch.

Mop was on his knees, weeding between the strawberry runners. I hadn't seen him since the bonfire. But that all seemed so long ago and unimportant.

He pushed back his curly hair and smudged dirt on his cheek. "Not mad at me?"

"No."

"It's so awful about Mr. Doyle, isn't it?"

I snipped parsley. "Do you know why those detectives are talking to Mr. Bains?"

"They've been looking around. They want to know if there are any foxgloves growing in the garden here."

He tossed a handful of dandelion roots into the wheelbarrow.

"Are there?"

"No. I wonder why they care about foxgloves."

"I don't know," I lied.

~&~

It was Saturday morning. We sat on leather chairs around the polished oak table in the library. Mr. Timmins was at the head, with a briefcase in front of him. A woman sat opposite him. I had seen her at dinner last night, sitting with Henry and Mr. Timmins.

"Why is Charlotte here?" said Henry.

"I asked her to come," said Mr. Timmins. "Charlotte, this is Mrs. Carpenter. She is Mr. Doyle's sister."

"How nice to meet you, Charlotte," she said. "Mr. Timmins told me how good you were to my brother."

She wasn't as elegant as Mrs. Chisholm and some of the other ladies at the St. Alice. She wore a navy blue dress and had dark auburn hair piled high on her head.

Mr. Timmins opened his briefcase and took out a sheet of cream paper. He pulled out a pair of spectacles from his waistcoat pocket and set them on his nose. "This is Jacob Doyle's will. I've waited until the three of you could be brought together as you are the beneficiaries."

So he *did* leave me his chess set. We'd never played that second game. The back of my eyes burned.

Mr. Timmins began to read. *"This is the last Will and Testament of me, Jacob Walter Doyle, of Victoria in the province of British Columbia in Canada."*

I looked at Henry. He was watching Mr. Timmins closely.

"I hereby revoke any and all other wills I have previously made," continued Mr. Timmins. *"I appoint my solicitor, Philip James Timmins, to be the sole Executor and Trustee of this my will. I direct my Trustee to pay all my just debts and funeral expenses."*

I imagined that Mr. Doyle was in the room with us, and it was his voice we were listening to.

"*I direct my Trustee to make the following bequests. I leave the sum of ten thousand dollars to my son Musa Kumalo. I leave the sum of ten thousand dollars to Henry Carter, son of my beloved friend Fanny Michelle Carter.*"

He hesitated. "*I leave the sum of ten thousand dollars to my daughter Charlotte O'Dell.*"

Chapter Thirty-four

My daughter, Charlotte O'Dell.

A roaring noise filled my head.

Henry jumped to his feet. "Daughter?"

"Calm yourself, Henry," said Mr. Timmins.

"You told me your father was killed in an accident in Toronto," said Henry.

"He was...I mean..." My throat closed and I couldn't speak.

"The man Charlotte knew as her father, Arthur O'Dell, raised her," said Mr. Timmins. "Jacob Doyle was her biological father."

"How long had he known that?" said Henry.

"This is not your concern, Henry. Charlotte, this must come as a great shock. We'll discuss this later in private."

"Musa Kumalo," said Mrs. Carpenter. "That's an African name. Jacob always was one for secrets. I must say, this is all a complete surprise to me. My brother having two children!"

"Secrets!" said Henry. "Is that what we're going to call this? A secret?"

I squeezed my hands together. My head was swimming.

"We'll order some tea," said Mrs. Carpenter. "This is too much of a shock for all of us."

"I would like to finish first," said Mr. Timmins. "Are you able to go on, Charlotte?"

I nodded.

"*I make these bequests in the understanding that these monies will be* used to further Henry's and Charlotte's and Musa's educations and any other purposes the trustee deems fit. If any of Henry or Charlotte or Musa are under the age of majority, the trustee will have the absolute discretion to use the monies for the benefit of such person until he or she reaches the age of majority."

I couldn't listen any longer. I couldn't think.

"I bequeath the residue of my estate to my sister Marion Carpenter of San Francisco. In testimony whereof I have to this day my last Will and Testament written upon these pages subscribed my name Jacob Walter Doyle this May 30 1908."

The silence in the room seemed to go on forever. I wanted Lizzie!

"This will?" said Henry. "He made it here at the hotel on May 30? That's the day he died. Is it legal?"

"It is absolutely legal," said Mr. Timmins. "It was properly witnessed by two guests, Mr. and Mrs. Howard. If challenged it will stand up in any court."

"What the hell does that mean about the age of majority?"

"The money for you and Charlotte and Musa will be held by me until you are twenty-one. Before then, it will be up to me how much to give you and for what purpose. The money for education will be available immediately. Musa is of course in a boarding school now. Mr. Doyle spoke at length of his wishes for you to go to university in September, Henry, and for Charlotte to finish her education. That is all possible with this inheritance."

"Gracious me, we need that tea," said Mrs. Carpenter. "Strong, with lots of sugar!" She sprang out of her chair and came to me, folding me into a huge hug. "My dear girl, this is marvellous news for you. It's terribly exciting! You'll realize that when it all sinks in."

Henry left, slamming the door.

"Charlotte, I'd like to speak with you alone," said Mr. Timmons.

I left Mr. Timmins and found Lizzie in the dining room, rolling napkins and tucking them in their silver holders. "Outside! Now!"

We sat beside the garbage bins behind the kitchen.

"Tell me everything," said Lizzie.

"We did the reading of the will and then Mr. Timmins talked to me by myself."

I stopped, suddenly too overcome to speak.

"And?"

"Mr. Doyle left me ten thousand dollars. He said I'm his daughter!"

"His daughter? You *had* a father. You're an O'Dell!"

"I know. But Mr. Timmins said that Mr. Doyle and my mother used to be sweethearts. Before I was born. Mr. Doyle thought it might be her when I showed him my parents' photograph. Then he recognized my brooch right away. He said he gave it to her!"

"They were lovers?"

"I don't know."

"Just *suppose* it's true. What else did Mr. Timmins say?"

"He said that Mr. Doyle knew my mother was pregnant."

"So then why didn't he marry her?"

"He wanted to but she wouldn't. She went to Toronto on a train. She didn't tell anyone where she was going. Mr. Timmins said Mr. Doyle even hired a detective but he couldn't find us."

"*If* this is true."

"Mr. Timmins thinks my father, I mean Arthur O'Dell, probably adopted me after he married my mother."

"So Mr. Timmins believes it."

"Yes."

"Do you?"

"I just don't know."

Lizzie sighed. "Ten thousand dollars!"

"You won't tell the other girls, will you?"

"No." Lizzie hugged me. "What are you going to do?"

"I'm sending a telegram to Aunt Ginny. Mr. Timmins is helping me. It's going to say *"Did Arthur O'Dell adopt me?"*

Chapter Thirty-five

"I behaved like an ass yesterday when Timmins read the will," said Henry. "Forgive me?"

We sat on a bench beside the lake, far enough down the boardwalk that Mrs. Bannerman wouldn't see me.

"It was just such a shock," said Henry.

"It was a shock to me, too."

"I always thought I was like Uncle Jacob's son. And now I find out he has a real son." He gave me a rueful smile. "And a daughter."

Maybe a daughter, I thought.

"You're shivering." Henry took off his coat. "This damned wind. Does it ever stop blowing? God, I've had a hellish day, trying to take this all in."

He took a cigarette out of his pocket, cupped his hand around it and lit it.

"I've got to go back," I said.

"Wait." Henry picked up my hand. "You know what? I think you should quit this crummy job and we'll run off together to Spain with our riches!"

"Mr. Timmins would have something to say about that!"

"Mr. Timmins is a bore. So what are you going to do then?"

"Go back to school."

Henry blew out a stream of smoke. "Whatever for?"

Lizzie and I slipped outside the kitchen door.

"Just when I start to like Henry again," I said, "he says something idiotic."

"What does he think? That he should go to his fancy school and education's not important to you?"

Annie stuck her head out the door. "There you are. Mrs. Bannerman was just here, looking for you, Charlotte. She said she can't understand why you're not in the kitchen at this time of day."

"Now what have I done?"

I expected a lecture, but Mrs. Bannerman just picked up a yellow envelope from her desk and handed it to me. "I trust your aunt has not gone missing again."

My fingers trembling, I opened the envelope. Did Arthur O'Dell adopt me?

I unfolded the paper.

One word.

Yes.

In the kitchen, I whispered the news to Lizzie.

"Oh, Char. Are you glad?"

"I just don't know."

"No time for chatting, girls," said Mrs. Wiggs. "We've got a dining room full of hungry guests."

The door opened. It was Gertie, looking terrified. "Those detectives are back. They're searching Charlotte and Lizzie's room. And Mrs. Bannerman says Charlotte's to go to Mr. Brown's office right away."

"Land's sake," said Mrs. Wiggs. "Mr. Wiggs says I won't get a moment's peace until this is settled. You better go, Charlotte."

Chapter Thirty-six

I waited in Mr. Brown's office, sick at the thought of the detectives searching our room. Lizzie and I had very few belongings but they were ours.

"Charlotte," said Detective Bentley. I jumped. The detectives had slipped in quietly behind me.

"We have the results from the blue bottle," said Detective Bentley. "A mixture of tonic water and quinine."

"What's quinine?" I said.

"The standard treatment for malaria. It comes from the bark of a tree in South America. It didn't show up in Mr. Doyle's autopsy so I highly doubt he took any of it."

"So Sing Lee was telling the truth."

"So it seems," said Detective Quinn.

Relief flooded me. I started to stand.

"Sit down," said Detective Quinn. "When did you first meet Mr. Doyle?"

"What? I...about a month ago. I don't remember the exact day he came."

"Oh, we know exactly when Mr. Doyle came to the hotel. May 4. But you met him months before, didn't you. You met him in Victoria."

"No!"

"How did you find out he was your father? Did he come to see you and that disappearing aunt of yours? Did he come to Buttercup House? Your aunt struggles to get by. And then one day this wealthy gentleman shows up, claiming to be your father. Did he suggest to your aunt that he would be leaving you some money in his will? Did your aunt help you plan his murder?"

"No! No. He never came to Buttercup House."

"It was a coincidence, was it?" continued Detective Quinn. "You and Mr. Doyle at the same hotel? I don't believe in coincidences, Charlotte."

"I never met him before. I didn't know he was my father until yesterday."

"Let's talk about yesterday. The reading of the will. You knew you were going to be a beneficiary. You and your aunt counted on that, didn't you?"

"That's not true."

"We think it is. Were the foxgloves your aunt's idea? Did she suggest you put it in the tea? Oh yes, we know all about your teas. You brought Mr. Doyle his tea. Special tea that you made yourself. How would a girl like you know how to make tea from plants in the garden?"

How did he find out about my teas? Who told him? *Glenys,* I thought. She had seen me making tea for Lizzie and for Mr. Doyle and she had told the detectives. I remembered Lizzie saying on my first day, *You don't want Glenys for an enemy.*

Both detectives watched me. "My aunt taught me."

"It was clever," said Detective Quinn. "At first give him just enough to make him ill, to make everyone think it was malaria. Mr. Doyle – pardon me, your *father* – liked his tea. He especially liked the fact that you made it just for him."

"Not just Mr. Doyle," I protested. "I made tea for other people, for Lizzie when she wasn't feeling well, and she didn't get sick."

"In the world of the police," said Detective Quinn, "we talk of two things. Motive and means. You have the motive. Ten thousand dollars is a fortune to a waitress. The means was the tea. You can go back to the kitchen, Charlotte. For now."

I barely listened as Annie talked about a new calf born on their farm that morning. Flora and Ina chatted in the scullery and Mrs. Wiggs scolded Glenys for letting the butter go too soft. The clatter of pots and pans sounded far away. Lizzie squeezed my arm.

Glenys said, "I never thought I'd be working with a criminal."

"I'll have no drama in my kitchen," said Mrs. Wiggs. "Charlotte's only helping the police with their enquiries. This will all blow over soon and we'll be back to normal."

She hadn't heard Detective Quinn's voice.

The door opened and the detectives stepped into the room. I put my hand out to steady myself on the edge of the table.

"Well, I never," said Mrs. Wiggs. "How am I supposed to get lunch on the table with all this –"

Detective Quinn took a step toward me. Everything around me went very still. "Charlotte O'Dell, I am arresting you for the murder of Jacob Doyle."

Chapter Thirty-seven

Detective Quinn waited at the bottom of the stairs.

I changed into a plain brown dress. My fingers fumbled when I tried to fasten my buttons and Lizzie had to do them.

"Please stop crying," I said. "You'll make me cry too. And now listen. This is important."

Lizzie nodded.

"Talk to Mr. Timmins. He'll know what to do."

Lizzie wiped her eyes. "I will."

"Henry's out walking again. You must tell him what happened."

"Come on, girl!" Detective Quinn shouted up the stairs.

"I can't walk," I said to Lizzie.

"I'll come with you."

"Take her out the back door," said Mr. Brown. "And Lizzie, go back to the kitchen."

Detective Bentley's motor car was parked behind the hotel. Detective Quinn slid into the front seat and Detective Bentley helped me into the back. "Your first trip in a motor car?"

"I've been in the omnibus. But I've never been in a motor car."

Detective Bentley got in behind the steering wheel. As we jolted forward, I gripped the edge of the seat.

"We're going to Mission," said Detective Bentley. "It's on the other side of the mountain."

We climbed and climbed. We stopped on the side of the road and the detectives took out packets of sandwiches and ate them.

"Would you like one?" said Detective Bentley.

I shook my head. The smell of garlicky sausage made me ill. A black fly landed on my cheek and I slapped it away.

After that, I lost all track of time. When we arrived in Mission, I stared numbly at the dusty street and the scattered wooden buildings. Two men, talking in front of a building with a sign that said *Royal Bank*, watched us pass.

We stopped in front of a low building with a Union Jack on a pole at the front.

"The jail," said Detective Quinn. "A night or two in here and you'll tell us the truth."

As I stepped out of the motor car, everything spun. My knees buckled.

~

Detective Bentley held a glass of water to my lips. "You fainted but you're all right now."

I was sitting on a bench in a small room. A man behind a messy desk stared at me. He was eating a boiled egg and bits of yellow yolk were scattered across his chest.

"You've been expecting us," said Detective Quinn.

"But she's just a girl," said the man.

"Don't be fooled. She knew what she was doing."

Detective Quinn turned to me. "Don't think this jailer is going to do you any favours."

My knees were like jelly again.

"Put your head down," said Detective Bentley. "Breathe... Better?"

"Yes," I whispered.

"We're leaving now," said Detective Quinn.

"Wait a minute." Detective Bentley crouched beside me. "Charlotte, there are people trying to help you."

My eyes welled up.

Dimly I heard the door shut. The jailer picked up a ring of jangling keys and heaved himself to his feet. "This beats all." He squinted at me. "Can you stand?"

"I think so."

I used the wall to steady myself. He held my arm and led me through a door into a narrow passageway, lit by an oil lamp that hung from the ceiling by a chain.

"I'll put you in here." He pushed open a door with bars. I half fell inside the cell. The door clanged and he turned a key. Through a blur of tears, I saw a thin mattress and a grey blanket on a low wooden shelf. In the corner was a tin bucket with a wooden lid.

The brick walls swirled and I grabbed a bar. Then I heard Detective Bentley's voice. He hadn't left me after all.

"It will be full of lice," he said. "She can't stay here."

Chapter Thirty-eight

I waited in a small warm kitchen while Detective Bentley, Detective Quinn and a woman talked in another room.

I heard the woman say, "Why did you bring her here? Don't we have a jail?"

Detective Bentley's words were muffled. I tried to calm myself by thinking about Aunt Ginny and Buttercup House.

The kitchen door opened. "This is my wife, Mrs. Bentley," said Detective Bentley. "She'll take care of you. Detective Quinn and I are going into the back room to read over the notes of the case."

Mrs. Bentley was a tall woman with grey hair coiled tightly around her head. She studied me.

"Are you hungry?" she said.

"No," I said.

"Do you want tea?"

"No."

"Do you need to use the outhouse?"

"No."

She sighed. "The best thing is to put you in our Steven's room. He's away at the logging camp at the end of Harrison Lake for the summer."

The small room next to the kitchen had a narrow bed and a rag rug on the floor.

"You can sleep in your dress," said Mrs. Bentley. "I'll say goodnight then."

I slid under a cold clammy sheet and pulled up a blanket. I stared at the ceiling, my eyes wide.

I heard Mrs. Bentley call the detectives for dinner. Then the scrape of chairs on the floor and the clatter of dishes. A kettle whistled.

What was going to happen to me? They hanged Mary Ansell for poisoning her sister. They would hang me too.

"We'll be off now," said Detective Bentley. "We want to get back to the St. Alice before dawn."

"I am going to lock her door," said Mrs. Bentley.

I buried my face in the pillow to muffle my sobs.

~

I heard a key turn in the lock.

Mrs. Bentley came into the room. "You've slept most of the day. There's someone here to see you."

A cold pit opened in my stomach. Who could it be? I stumbled into the kitchen. Mr. Timmins stood by the door.

I burst into tears.

"I'm taking you back to the St. Alice, Charlotte," he said. "Thank you, Mrs. Bentley, for everything."

Mrs. Bentley nodded.

It was drizzling outside. Mr. Timmins settled me into the front seat of his motor car. "You're free now, Charlotte. Why don't you lean back and close your eyes. We can talk later."

I started crying again. Mr. Timmins pulled a white handkerchief from his pocket and passed it to me.

"I want to know what happened now," I said.

"It's really because of Mrs. Bannerman. She sent Mr. Doyle's shirts to the wash house to be laundered. Sally found a piece of paper in one of the pockets. She gave it to Mrs. Bannerman. She knew right away what it was. A receipt for a prescription for digitalis from a doctor in

Victoria. She went to Detective Bentley immediately."

"So he *was* taking digitalis!"

"I showed Dr. Herman the receipt. He was very puzzled. He couldn't understand why he didn't find any digitalis in Mr. Doyle's room. We decided that I should talk to Effie."

"Because she's the one who cleaned his room."

"Exactly. As soon as she saw me, she broke down. It took a while to get the whole story. The morning Mr. Doyle died, she knocked a bottle off his night table and broke it. She was so afraid of getting into trouble, she hid the pieces in her room. I think she was quite relieved to get them for me. I gave them to Detective Bentley and Detective Quinn. With some difficulty, they were able to read the label and confirm that it was from the pharmacy in Victoria and was indeed digitalis."

It was so much to follow.

"So what does that mean?"

"It means it's possible that no one poisoned Mr. Doyle. That he mixed up his dosage and took too much."

"It proves I'm innocent, then."

"Not exactly," said Mr. Timmins. "It creates doubt in the eyes of the police. "Enough doubt to let you go. Of course, *I* know you're innocent –"

"But not everyone will."

"The police have closed the case as an accidental overdose."

"Do you believe that?"

"No. Mr. Doyle was not a careless man."

"I don't believe it either."

"Then you and I, Charlotte, may be the only ones who know that there's a murderer still out there."

Chapter Thirty-nine

Lizzie poured me a scalding bath. I soaked until the water turned lukewarm, scrubbing my skin with a washcloth. I washed my hair and rinsed it over and over again.

Lizzie had smuggled up egg sandwiches and a pot of tea. I devoured the sandwiches in huge unlady-like bites. "Where's Henry?"

"He left," said Lizzie. "This afternoon."

"Did you talk to him before he went?"

"No."

"Did he leave a message for me?"

"No. But Mop wants to see you. He's been so upset."

"Not now."

I lay on my bed in my clean underclothes.

"I've got to go lay the tables for morning," said Lizzie. "I'll try to bring some more food."

I closed my eyes. In a few minutes, she was back. "Mr. Brown wants you. Oh Char, he's in an awful temper."

My heart pounded as I struggled into my uniform.

Mr. Brown was waiting in his office. "There you are!"

He waved the front page of the *British Colonist* in my face.

I stared at the headline.

WAITRESS AT ST. ALICE POISONS GUEST.

"It's all over Victoria by now!" Mr. Brown's eyes bulged. "The reputation of the St. Alice is ruined!"

"But I'm innocent."

"Your employment here is over."
I was sacked.

VICTORIA

1908

Chapter Forty

"You're safe now, Charlotte," said Aunt Ginny. "You're home in Buttercup House where you belong."

"The worse part was saying goodbye to Lizzie," I gasped through my tears. "Even worse than that jail."

Mr. Chang banged his cane on the kitchen floor. "I don't like the sound of that policeman. If he were here, I'd soon set him straight."

"Why don't you unpack your suitcase, dear," said Aunt Ginny, "while I make some tea."

"Imagine our Charlotte being an heiress," said Mr. Chang

"I'm going to be a pharmacist," I called through my bedroom doorway.

"That's all very well for the future," said Aunt Ginny. "Lavender with a touch of lemon balm. It will calm our nerves."

In the morning, I buttoned my shoes and grabbed a warm scone from the kitchen table.

"Where are you off to so early?" said Aunt Ginny.

"The cemetery." My eyes filled with tears. "I don't know what's the matter with me."

"I wanted you to stay in bed this morning."

Mr. Chang looked up from his newspaper. "We'll play a game of chess when you get back."

I would never play chess again.

"I might be a long time."

I picked daisies in the meadow behind Buttercup House. I put them in Rosemary's basket and pedaled down the road. I wheeled my bike through the iron gates.

The cemetery was deserted. Tiny lacy spiderwebs sparkled in the dewy grass. On top of a bush, a sparrow burst into song. I walked along a wide gravel path, shaded by tall trees, to my parents' headstone. I laid the daisies on the grass and sat on a bench. I touched my brooch and at last felt peaceful.

I left Rosemary by the headstone. For the next hour, I wandered through the cemetery, reading names and dates and musing about their lives. I gazed at tall stone crosses and monuments with garlands carved on the sides and big stone urns.

I turned onto a narrow path that soon dwindled into scrubby grass and weeds. I was in a part of the cemetery I had never seen before. Many of the headstones were tilted or had fallen to the ground. The trees were huge and the air cool in their shade.

I read the words on a small plain gravestone, partly sunken in the grass.

Joseph Charles Edwards
February 10, 1853 to June 16, 1853

A baby.

How sad. The silly tears welled up again. I walked over to a huge stone angel and gazed up. Her eyes were downcast and her carved hair flowed over her shoulders. The tip of one wing lay broken in the long grass. I knelt down, pulled away the weeds and touched her chipped bare feet.

I heard someone shouting.

I looked up. Two women were standing by a grove of oak trees. One was leaning on a cane and dressed in black mourning. I caught my breath.

Bertrand Carter's mother. Stella.

The other woman wore a green suit and a bowler hat with feathers. *Mrs. Chisholm.* How could that be?

Stella moved closer to Mrs. Chisholm until they were almost touching. Her voice rose to a scream. "I'll tell you when it's over!"

Mrs. Chisholm put her hands up. "Leave me alone!"

Stella's hand lashed out. I heard the crack of a slap across Mrs. Chisholm's cheek.

Heart pounding, I crouched behind the angel.

Mrs. Chisholm hurried past me, her head bent, sobbing.

I waited a long time, hardly daring to breathe. Listening for Stella. When I was sure she was gone, I made my way back along the winding paths to my parents' headstone. I pedaled furiously to the cemetery gates.

Stella and Mrs. Chisholm.

What had I seen? Stella *hated* Mr. Doyle. She wanted him dead. And Mrs. Chisholm was at the St. Alice when Mr. Doyle was murdered.

Ice ran down my back.

I had to tell Henry.

Saint Bartholomew's was closed for the summer. Henry had told me he would go back to Stella's house to sort his mother's things. I turned my bicycle onto the road to the Gorge.

The last house on the Gorge Road, Henry had said. *My mother hated it there. It was so isolated.*

I pedaled faster. The road closed in with dark trees, the houses scattered far apart.

I saw them from a distance. They grew in front of a tall house with a sooty chimney, its shingles stained black by the weather. Pale purple blooms waved in the breeze.

Foxgloves.

Chapter Forty-one

A mourning wreath of yew hung on the door. I banged my fist.

I heard footsteps. Henry opened the door. A sour smell hit me. Over his shoulder, I saw a dark entrance hall with closed doors on both sides.

"Charlotte! What are you *doing* here? I thought –"

"It was Stella and Mrs. Chisholm!"

"What?"

"They were in it together. They killed Mr. Doyle."

"Christ. Look, you better come in."

Henry shut the door. Dim light filtered through a window. It was gloomy, the walls covered with dark green flocked wallpaper. At one end rose a steep staircase, with threadbare carpet on each tread.

"I saw them at the cemetery. They were fighting."

"Who?"

"Mrs. Chisholm and Stella. Stella slapped Mrs. Chisholm. I *saw* them."

"Who the hell is Mrs. Chisholm?"

"A guest. She was at the St. Alice when Mr. Doyle was murdered."

"Murdered?" Henry stared at me. "You heard the Coroner. It was an overdose of digitalis that killed Uncle Jacob. An accidental overdose."

"The Coroner was wrong. It was murder. Stella planned it. She hated Mr. Doyle. Henry, those are *foxgloves* growing in front of this house. She gave roots or the leaves to Mrs. Chisholm and somehow Mrs. Chisholm used them to poison Mr. Doyle."

139

"Why would she do that?"

"I don't know. But she was at the St. Alice the whole time Mr. Doyle was ill. Then she left the day after he died. And she knows Stella. It's the only thing that makes sense. It fits."

"Jesus. Let me *think*."

I took huge breaths to steady myself.

"Even if you're right," said Henry at last, "we'll never be able to prove it."

"Tell me everything you know about Stella."

"She's insane."

He paced back and forth.

"She's in this house all by herself. The maid and cook are gone. She sits for hours in Carter's room. Not the room he shared with my mother. His old room."

"What's she doing in there?"

"Talking to Carter. I heard her last night through the walls. All night long. It was awful. And she dragged something across the floor. It sounded heavy."

"A desk maybe?"

"Could be. Or even the bed."

"She's hiding something," I said.

"What?"

"I don't know. But whatever it is, it could connect her to Mrs. Chisholm and Mr. Doyle's murder."

"She keeps Carter's room locked, but I know where she hides the key. We have to go fast. She could be back any minute."

Henry took me into a dark cramped kitchen.

"God, it stinks in here." He reached up to a shelf above the sink and lifted down an orange tin that said *Rowntree's Cocoa*. He pulled off the lid and took out a black iron key.

At the top of the steep staircase, he struggled with the lock. "Damn!

I know it's the right key."

The key turned and the lock clicked. He pushed the door open.

Men's blue striped pajamas and a brown flannel dressing gown lay across a four poster bed. Worn leather slippers were placed neatly on the floor. An ivory comb, a crystal bottle with a silver cap, a pocket watch and gold cufflinks sat on top of a heavy wood dresser.

"It's like a shrine in here," I said.

Henry crossed the floor to an open window. Filmy curtains blew back into the room. He thrust his head out the window. "I don't see her."

There was a straight-backed chair beside a small table. I picked up a photograph in a silver frame. A man wearing a black suit stared at me with cold eyes.

She's talking to Carter, Henry had said. I shuddered and put it back on the table.

"That gouge in the floor in front of the dresser," said Henry. "That's what she was dragging."

He grabbed the corner, pulled it away from the wall, and crouched down. "There's a door back here."

I knelt beside him. "A cubbyhole?"

Henry tugged on a small white knob and the square door fell forward and banged the back of the dresser. He reached his hand inside. "There's something here." He passed me a brown leather pouch tied with a thin leather cord.

"There's something else." He rocked back. "Here." He handed me a black book with gilt-edged pages.

"It's a Bible." I dropped the Bible on the bed. I untied the pouch and turned it upside down. Bundles of bills tied with string spilled onto the bedspread.

"There's a bloody fortune here," said Henry. "Where did she get it?"

He started stuffing the bills back into the pouch. "We've got to go!"

"Wait!" I picked up the Bible. "There's something stuck in here."

I opened the book and turned the thin tissue pages. I stopped. A piece of heavier paper, one edge torn, had been glued over the Bible page. Across the middle was written in black ink:

The Diary of Miranda Dutton

Miranda. That was Mrs. Chisholm's name.

I felt a sudden chill. I turned the page over. It was puckered and crackled with dried glue. Another paper glued in, the edges ragged.

July 4, 1859
Today I killed my mother

Chapter Forty-two

"Miranda's mother was going to fire me."

Stella stepped into the room, her mourning dress rustling. Her face was a skull, white skin stretched tight over her bones, her eyes sunken. "Randi. That's what I called Miranda. She did everything I told her to do. She still will. She's weak."

She pulled a small silver gun from the folds of her dress.

"*Christ*," said Henry.

I stared at the gun. My heart crashed into my ribs.

"For six months I was a maid in their house. Randi was afraid of her mother. That's how I controlled her."

She's insane, Henry had said.

"One night, her mother came to my room. She accused me of stealing. A pearl necklace. Emerald earrings. *You'll never work again in London*, she said. *Never. Leave my house. Now!* She turned to go back down the stairs. Randi was on the landing. Listening. Sniveling."

Stella's thin lips pulled back in a smile. "*Push her*, I said. And she did."

Bile rose in my throat.

"Police came to the house. Randi was hysterical. I threatened her, told her to keep her mouth shut. The stupid girl kept a dairy. I'd seen it in her jewelry box. I had to know what she wrote. I watched the house. She left one morning with her father and I slipped inside and got it. *Today I killed my mother.* Nothing about me. The little fool."

She took a step forward. I shrank back, pressing into Henry.

"I get rid of people who cross me. Miranda's mother. And Jacob Doyle."

She raised the gun and pointed it at us.

"Please God. No," I whispered.

"Doyle betrayed my son. I read the letter first and I gave it to Bertrand. *Finally you know what kind of woman you've married*, I said. *A whore*. He went up the stairs. *Fanny! Where are you, Fanny?* he shouted. Fanny was in the parlour. She knew what she'd done. I heard Bertrand slamming doors. I got my gun from my writing desk and followed him. He was in his room. *You have no choice*, I said. *Shoot her.*"

"You bitch," said Henry.

"He wouldn't do it. Coward. *I'm leaving*, he said. *I'm taking Fanny with me if she'll have me. We should have gone years ago.*"

Spittle flecked the corners of her lips. "I did everything for him. Everything. *You're the reason she had an affair, mother, he said. You drove her to it. You can stay here at the Gorge and rot by yourself.*"

I watched in horror the tears sliding down her ashen cheeks.

"And then I shot him."

"You shot your *son?*" said Henry.

"Fanny heard the shot. She came running and knelt beside him. Right there beside that bed. She looked up at me. I saw it in her eyes. Fear. And I shot her too."

Henry lunged towards her.

I screamed.

Hooves clattered outside the window. A delivery truck.

I ran to the sill. "Help! Somebody come!"

"No!" cried Henry.

Behind me, there was a deafening explosion.

Chapter Forty-three

Mr. Chang and I read the newspaper together.

SUICIDE AT THE GORGE

On June 9, an elderly woman shot herself in her home at the Gorge. Stella Carter was...

I stopped reading. I wanted to go outside. Breathe fresh air. Feel the sun.

For the next week, I cycled through the country lanes, desperate to forget the horror. At night, I tossed and turned and cried out. Aunt Ginny sent Mr. Chang to Sing Lee every day for different herbs and roots. She made me tinctures of St John's wort and yarrow and valerian.

But I couldn't shut out the sound of the gun.

One day, when I got back to Buttercup House, Aunt Ginny said, "Henry was here. He asked to meet you at the Dickens Café at three o'clock."

"Should I go?"

Aunt Ginny hugged me. "It might help you to put the matter to rest."

∿

I sat at a table in the corner of the café.

"Tea, Miss?" said an older women with a tired face.

"A glass of water, please. I'm waiting for someone."

I sipped my water and watched the door. It swung open and a

heavy-set man came inside.

Detective Bentley.

He waved and walked over to my table. "What a nice surprise. May I sit for a minute?"

I nodded and he lowered himself into a chair. "What a dreadful business at the Gorge."

"Is that why you've come to Victoria?"

"Yes. I'm assisting the police here."

"They've talked to Henry and me for hours. They keep going over and over the same things. Do you think they'll arrest Mrs. Chisholm?"

"She has denied everything. And now with Stella Carter dead..." He rubbed his jaw. "There's so much we'll never know."

"Why did Mrs. Chisholm do it?"

"Blackmail."

"The money in the pouch?"

"Yes. There's no doubt that Stella was blackmailing her."

"Stella was there when Mrs. Chisholm pushed her mother down the stairs and she had the page from the diary to prove it."

"That's right. We know that Miranda's father sent her to his cousin in Victoria. Stella and young Bertrand came fifteen years later in 1874. Mrs. Chisholm was married by then and frequently written about in the newspaper. It's likely that Stella saw her photograph and recognized her. We don't know when the blackmail started."

"She kept that page from the diary all these years, hidden in the Bible," I said.

Detective Bentley nodded. "She knew it would be a powerful weapon one day. We've sent telegrams back and forth to the police in London. They have an old record of a Mrs. Dutton dying after a fall down the stairs in her home in Chelsea. *Accident*, it said at the bottom. But there was something else."

"What?"

"Someone had scribbled a note in pencil in the margin of the file. *Look at the maid.*"

I felt a chill. "Will the police in London want to talk to Mrs. Chisholm?"

"No, the case is closed."

"How did Stella find out that Mr. Doyle was taking digitalis?"

"We talked to the nurse who works for Mr. Doyle's doctor. She admitted that Stella befriended her and that she may have been indiscreet and said too much."

"Stella never knew they killed the wrong Jacob."

Detective Bentley shook his head. "In so many ways, it's a tragic case."

I leaned forward. "It was the marmalade. Mr. Doyle had special marmalade from Scotland. He kept it in his room. They were talking about the marmalade on the verandah and Mrs. Chisholm was there. Mr. Doyle never locked his door. She could have slipped in and put foxglove in the marmalade."

Detective Bentley frowned. "I don't recall a jar of marmalade when we searched his room."

"I washed it out the morning he died."

Detective Bentley shook his head. "It would be hard to prove without evidence."

"You didn't need much evidence to arrest me."

He raised his hands.

"It was Glenys' fault. She told you I made teas for Mr. Doyle."

"Glenys?"

"The kitchen maid. She told you when you interviewed her."

"No, not Glenys. It was the young man. Henry."

"Henry? Are you sure?"

"Oh yes. He asked to speak to us. He said it was important. It couldn't wait. It was damning evidence. He had seen you make tea from garden plants for Mr. Doyle. With everything else, it made a strong case against you."

He stood up and shook my hand. "I wish you well, Charlotte. You have a wonderful life ahead of you."

I looked up at the clock. Five minutes to three.

I left the café.

VICTORIA

July 1920

HOT SPRINGS HOTEL DESTROYED BY FIRE

The St. Alice Hotel, Harrison Hot Springs, one of the oldest and best known hostelries in British Columbia, was totally destroyed by fire on Sunday. Starting, it is believed, from a defective flue, the flames were first noticed eating through the shingles on the roof.

In about an hour and a half, the big three-storey frame structure was represented only by a tottering chimney and a heap of glowing embers. Due largely to the fact that the outbreak of fire came when most of the guests were out of the building, there was fortunately no loss of life. Scenes of the wildest excitement prevailed for a couple of hours and it was an extremely difficult matter to check up on all the guests who, together with the residents around the Springs district, worked like Trojans in saving the contents of the venerable health resort. Most of the furniture and effects on the first floor were saved. The guests all rallied to the alarm, and practically all of them were able to force their way through the thick smoke to their rooms and save their personal belongings.

– From *The Daily Colonist*, July 20, 1920

Sipping my morning coffee, I'm shocked by the news. My coffee grows cold as I let my mind drift back to the events of 1908.

My life since that summer has had its ups and downs. Aunt Ginny made it to the age of ninety-one. I miss her every day. Mr. Chang still lives in Buttercup House. We play mahjong on Sunday afternoons. I saw Colonel Mitterand once, berating a shop keeper in Fan Tan Alley. I lost track of Henry but I heard that he was killed in the Great War and decorated posthumously with a Victoria Cross. Mrs. Chisholm, I read in the *Colonist*, died a recluse.

My husband Mop is my greatest supporter. We have decided not to have any children, and get great fulfillment from our life's work, me as a pharmacist in Victoria and Mop as head gardener at Butchart Gardens. We have lively discussions about the suffragette movement, which is dear to my heart.

Our kitchen clock strikes the hour. I fold the newspaper carefully because Mop left early for work and has not had a chance to read about the St. Alice.

I head upstairs to put on a suitable dress and tame my wild hair. Lizzie is reading from her novel at a bookstore on Yates Street. I don't want to be late.

The End

HISTORIC PHOTOGRAPHS

The St. Alice Hotel, a jewel in the wilderness.

Guests at the St. Alice Hotel.

The Omnibus

On the Road to the St. Alice Hotel

ACKNOWLEDGEMENTS

I would like to thank my editor, Kathy Stinson, who saw that I was on the wrong path and gently but firmly pointed me in the right direction! Also a heartfelt thanks to the amazing team at Coteau Books.

This book would never have been written without the inspiration of my dear friend and historian Bev Kennedy. Judy Pickward and Joan Vogstad at the Agassiz-Harrison Museum provided valuable assistance with my research. My sister Janet read many many drafts and helped make the mystery and characters come alive.

My wonderful husband Larry makes it possible for me to have the time to write.

AUTHOR'S NOTE:

In the interest of historical accuracy, I have used the words Indian and Chinaman, terms which are certainly inappropriate today.

ABOUT THE AUTHOR

Becky Citra is the author of over twenty books for young readers. Her most recent work with Coteau, *The Griffin of Darkwood* was nominated for the OLA® Silver Birch® Award, and was a finalist for the IODE Violet Downey Book Award. She has written two popular series – the *"Ellie and Max"* series which takes place in Upper Canada in the 1800's and the *Jeremy and the Enchanted Theater* time travel series. She currently lives in Bridge Lake, British Columbia, Canada.